CAPTURE THE NIGHT

THE ENFORCERS

JANE HINCHEY

BAYWOLF PRESS

AUTHOR'S NOTE

Welcome to "The Enforcers" series—a collection that has truly been on a remarkable journey. When I first embarked on this adventure, I could hardly have imagined the twists and turns it would take. Initially self-published under my own name, these stories found a new identity with the pen name Zahra Stone, and even underwent a title transformation along the way. Now, they've come full circle, returning to their original author.

While I'm predominantly known for my cozy mysteries, "The Enforcers" holds a special place in my heart. It's a series that has evolved with me and witnessed the various stages of my writing career. I'm thrilled to present these stories to you once more, enriched by their journey and under my own name again.

To stay updated with all my literary escapades, including the latest on "The Enforcers" and my cozy mysteries, I warmly invite you to sign up for my newsletter. It's the best way to keep in the loop about new releases and exclusive content.

You can sign up for my newsletter here:
Janehinchey.com/subscribe

Thank you for joining me on this incredible journey. I hope you enjoy the world of "The Enforcers" as much as I have enjoyed bringing it to you.

xoxo

Jane

ABOUT THIS BOOK

I'm Katie Shelton, and I've been running from my past long enough. As an agent for the Supernatural Intelligence Agency, I've masked my pain with sarcasm and a tough exterior. But now, duty calls me back to the town where it all fell apart, where memories of lost love and tragedy haunt every corner.

Enter Brax Lane, Secret Service agent and the kind of man who sees through my defenses. He's dangerously attractive, and as we're thrown together to investigate a sinister threat, the walls around my heart start to crumble.

Passion flares, tempting me with a future I never dared dream of again. But as danger looms, threatening my family and the town, I'm forced to confront my true nature as a fire demon. Harnessing my power means embracing the scars of my past, trusting Brax with the wounds I've kept hidden.

It's a race against time. Can I tap into my strength and allow love back into my life, or will the evil lurking in the shadows consume everything I hold dear? This is more than just a mission; it's my chance for redemption, for love, for a new beginning. Welcome to my story, where the flames of passion and peril burn equally bright.

Author's Note: The journey concludes with Capture the Night, which first greeted the world as Marked in Fire, part of the SIA series by Jane Hinchey. Under the pen name Zahra Stone, it transformed into Capture the Night, and now it returns to its roots. This edition, true to its origins, comes to you with minor enhancements, proudly bearing my name once more. Revisit this captivating narrative, where the essence of the tale endures, inviting you back to its magical depths for one last adventure.

Holding my breath, I slowly turned my head and studied the man sleeping next to me. He was sprawled on his stomach, his face turned toward me, and I couldn't help but admire the pure perfection of him. From the dark hair sweeping across his brow to the long eyelashes and sensual lips, he was put together just right, and my lady bits clenched in appreciation. Only one question. Who the hell was he?

Memories from last night came back to me in a rush, and I bit my lip to hold back the groan. I'd been at a bar. He was there. He bought me a drink. One thing led to another, and here we were. Only, who was he? All I knew was that he was a fire demon, like me. Initially, I'd been curious, but then it hadn't really mattered who or what he was. He was just a body. But now I had a pressing issue... how the hell do I get out of here without waking him up? I had zero interest in getting to know him despite the hot sex and his drop-dead good looks. This was a one-off, an aberration on my behalf, and I needed to get out of here before he started asking questions I didn't want to answer.

Biting back a curse, I slid out of bed as quietly as I could and tiptoed across the room, scooping up my clothes as I went. I debated for a second on how quietly I could dress. Would I inadvertently wake him? Was it safer to dress in the bathroom? But would the sound of the door opening and closing disturb him? All of these thoughts flashed through my mind, and I shifted my weight from one foot to the other, causing the floorboards to creak. I froze, eyes zeroing in on his face.

One eye cracked open, then the other. He blinked. Once, twice, then focused chocolate brown eyes on me.

"Going so soon?" he mumbled, rolling to his back and stretching, the sheet dipping low on his abdomen. *Fuck.*

"Errrr." I clutched my bundle of clothes and stood like a deer in the headlights. *Come on, Katie,* I scolded myself; get *your act together. You've got this. You are a strong, independent woman with nothing to be ashamed of.* I bit back a groan when he swung his legs out of bed and stood, gloriously unashamed of his naked body.

"Coffee?" he asked, crossing the room to where a coffee maker sat on the dresser. He flicked it on without waiting for a reply and disappeared into the bathroom.

I had about one minute to get my clothes on and get out of this hotel room. Dropping the bundle of clothes, I rummaged for my underwear, pulled them on, then my jeans, and was almost done when the toilet flushed. Breathless, I tugged my shirt over my head and heard the running of water. Then the door was opening. *Shit, shit, shit.* I scooped up my boots and headed for the door.

"Wait!" *Damn it.* I dropped my head, closing my eyes for a brief moment before straightening to face him.

"Yes?"

"I didn't get your name," he drawled, his lips curling in a seductive smirk, and while he'd wrapped a towel around his hips, the expanse of naked torso called to me. I had to bite my tongue to keep from licking him like I had last night. I almost groaned at the memory.

"I didn't give it." My voice came out breathless, and I saw his nostrils flare, sensing my arousal.

"Will I see you again?" His eyes were darker now, changing from hazel chocolate to almost black. He was as turned on as I was.

"Doubtful."

"Why?" He took a step toward me, and I held up my hand, palm toward him. He stopped. If he came closer, all my good intentions would fly out the window, and I couldn't let that happen. Last night had been a mistake. A great blow my fucking socks off mistake, but a mistake, nonetheless.

"It's just not a good idea. Look, thanks for a great night. I had fun. But this is goodbye." I opened the door, only to have it slammed shut. He'd moved fast and now stood behind me, one hand over my head, holding the door closed. I rested my forehead against it for a moment and breathed in the scent of him, felt my arousal climb, and knew I was scant seconds away from dragging him back to bed. He brushed his lips against the back of my neck, and god help me, I moaned.

"You want me." His voice was muffled against

my skin, but I heard the pure male pride in it. And the thread of determination.

"True. But it isn't going to happen." I screwed my eyes shut, trying to push down the riot of lust shooting through my body like a pinball machine on steroids. He froze behind me, and I almost laughed. An honorable man. He wouldn't force me, even though he knew it wouldn't take much to convince me to return to his bed.

"Why fight it? You want me; we both know I want you. What happened between last night and now? Regret?" His hot breath blew on the skin of my nape, and I shivered. *Regret?* No. I'd learned to live my life without regrets. More like self-preservation. There was something about him, something in our chemistry that told me he could be dangerous for me; he could tear down the walls I'd built around myself. He was a risk I wasn't prepared to take.

"Sorry, I've got to go. Work." I attempted to open the door again, heard him sigh behind me before removing his hand and letting me leave. I didn't turn back, didn't look at him again, just darted through the door, boots clutched to my chest, and kept going down the corridor toward the green exit sign. The silence was loud, and I didn't breathe until I heard the click of his door closing.

TWO

Putting two fingers in my mouth, I blew out an ear-piercing whistle. Silence descended as everyone turned and looked at me.

"Right! Listen up " I spun slowly, making eye contact with all of my family members gathered together in my parents' living room. "This is serious. Deadly serious. I need you to listen to me closely. Do not interrupt. There'll be time for questions when I've finished."

"But Katie—" my mom began, but I shushed her with a finger to my lips.

"No, Mom. Listen first. Please." The puzzled looks on their faces were priceless, but now wasn't the time for fun and games. Their lives were in danger, and their safety was my number one priority. I pushed down the inconvenient memory of last night when my number one priority had been sex with a stranger. It was because I was here back home in Maxxan. It had thrown me for a loop, and I was acting out of character, but there was no time to dwell on that now. I had to deal with the problem at hand. Saving their lives.

"We all know about fire demons, correct?" Considering my dad and uncles were all fire demons, and my brother and cousins gathered here today were part fire demon, this was no surprise to us. I knew what was coming would be news to them.

"And we know about vampires." They nodded, glancing at each other, then back at me, wondering where this was going.

"You probably don't know about ghouls, but they are out there. There are a lot of supernatural creatures out there that you don't know about."

"What's this about, Katie?" Dad demanded. I eyeballed him, and he crossed his arms over his chest, not pleased at being shushed by his daughter.

"Agent Jordan Buchanan introduced you to the Supernatural Intelligence Agency, the SIA. And, of course, he recruited Rae into the Agency. What you don't know is that I'm also an agent. I have been for three years. I'm what you call an enforcer—sort of like a detective in human terms."

"Sweet," my brother Cody murmured, looking impressed.

"And I've come home to protect you from a threat here in Maxxan." There was a rush of voices, each talking over the other as the shock of what I'd said hit them. I let them chatter for a moment before shushing them back into silence.

"What I'm about to tell you cannot be repeated outside of this room, understood? And I'm sharing this with you because your lives are in danger, and I convinced my boss... you remember the Director of the SIA, Nate Wilder? The one who won over our Paige? Yeah, he's my boss. Anyway, I have his permission to share this with you on the proviso it goes no further. I need your agreement on this."

I was barraged with a wave of *"yeah sure,"* *"okay,"* *"whatever."*

"There is a woman, a shifter called Keri Ridgeway, who is working with a ghoul to create a super paranormal. They're experimenting with drugs to do this. Up until recently, their experiments have failed, and the individuals they've experimented on have died. Ugly, painful deaths. But then they took Paige."

"What the hell!" Dad barked, jumping to his feet. "They took our daughter, and we weren't notified?"

"She's fine, Dad. We got her back. She's okay," I soothed, moving close and rubbing my hand up and down his back, then gently easing him back into his chair.

"But,"—I held up my hand to stop any more interruptions—"they did discover something when they had Paige. They discovered that Fire Demons could withstand the drug they were developing. We rescued Paige and shut down their operation in Redmeadows; however, they were using a legitimate pharmaceutical company as a front, and that pharmaceutical company has a factory and distribution center here."

"You think they're here? In Maxxan?" My cousin Cameron asked.

"We do. And they know the Shelton's are part fire demon." I let that sink in for a moment. "Since they no longer have Paige, we're pretty sure they'll be trying to get their hands on another fire demon and continue with their experiments. The SIA can't allow that to happen. And on a personal level, I can't let that happen." I couldn't hide the sudden hitch in my voice.

"Katie." This time it was Mom who rose and enveloped me in a hug.

"It's okay, Mom. I'm okay. I'm here to do a job—shut these bastards down once and for all—but I can't do that and protect all of you at the same time."

Cody nodded. "You have a plan."

"Yes. So, Mom, Aunt Deb, and Aunt Martha? You're human, and while you think you're not at risk because you're not a fire demon, you could be taken and used as bait to capture any one of us. So, we need to get you out of town, away from all this. Nate and Paige want you to go and stay with them in Redmeadows—seriously, you'll love it. Nate has a *mansion*! You'll be protected there, more than what I can offer you here."

The three women looked at each other and started nodding. Good. I had them on board.

"And the rest of us?" my cousin Tyler asked.

"You can go to Redmeadows as well. As I said, Nate has a mansion and can house all of you. Or you can stay here on the proviso that you take training—proper training—on how to use your fire demon skills and some basic self-defense training. Our number one priority is not having any of you taken. You need to be aware and on guard one hundred percent of the time. If you can't do that, you need to leave."

"How long?"

"How long do you need to stay away?" I shrugged. "We don't know. A few days at the least, a couple of weeks at the most. It's impossible to say."

Uncle Glenn cleared his throat. "I'll go to Redmeadows. I'm not leaving Martha on her own, and it'll give us a chance to catch up with the kids." Aunt Martha smiled at her husband and linked her fingers with his, squeezing. Their children, my twin cousins Vanessa and Travis, ran an Advertising Agency in Redmeadows, and we had the SIA keeping an eye on them there.

"Love? Do you want me to stay or go?" Dad asked Mom, who smiled at him in such a loving way I had to avert my eyes.

"You stay, hon. I'll take Deb with me, and we'll go see Paige. Cody, will you be coming with us?" she asked my brother.

"Nah, I'm staying. Tyler and Cameron? Going or staying?" he asked in turn.

"Staying," they said in unison, but then I'd known they would. They had lives here in Maxxan. Cameron had his garage, and Tyler was studying medicine. Which led me to Tyler's girlfriend, Sophie. She was human. She could be a problem.

"Before you ask, Sophie and I broke up. A while ago," Tyler offered. "She doesn't need to be involved in this, does she?"

"I'll check with HQ," I told him. "Does she know you're a fire demon?" He shook his head.

"Okay, so Aunt Deb, Aunt Martha, Uncle Glenn, and Mom—you're all going to Redmeadows, correct?" They all agreed.

"That leaves Dad, Cody, Cameron, and Tyler staying here."

"What about Rae?" Cameron asked. "Is my sister coming home?"

"She'll be assigned here. Even though she's still in training, she knows the people and the area. We'll take any advantage we can get." I blew out a relieved breath. They had all taken this better than I'd expected. Now came the tricky part.

"One last thing." I paused, sucking in a breath. "Grandma's house."

"What about it?" Mom asked.

"Grandma left it to Rae with some terms attached to it. Rae has approved for the SIA to convert it into our Maxxan headquarters...provided you agree?" I looked to my brother and cousins, for the house had been left to all of us grandchildren, on the proviso Rae didn't want it.

"Vanessa and Travis are okay with it, as is Paige. The ownership will not change hands; it'll still be Rae's place—our place—the SIA will be our tenant, but changes will be made, like bedrooms turned into offices, proper cells constructed in the cave underneath, that type of thing. The SIA will cover any construction or renovation costs."

When they all readily agreed, including my parents and aunt and uncle, I was surprised. We'd put such strong stock in the family property that I'd thought they'd want to hold on to the house. Emotions had run high when Grandma had died and the will had been read. Rae had been furious she'd been backed into a corner with the house being left to her, that she had to live in it for a year to retain ownership. If she left, the house would sit empty for a year and then be sold. Lost to the family forever. Thankfully, that had all turned out okay in the end, and the Shelton family still retained the property.

I wrapped up the meeting. "Those of you going to Redmeadows need to leave today. Go home, pack some stuff, and head to the airport. There's a charter plane waiting. Nate will have a car waiting for you at the other end that will take you to his home. The rest of you? Report to Rae's place at eight a.m. tomorrow for training. In the meantime, double, triple-check your locks, be aware of your surroundings, and check that no one is following you. If you suspect something is off, call me. Even if it's a false alarm, call me regardless. You do not want to be taken by these people."

THREE

"Holy hairy dog balls...is that? Katie Shelton?"

I froze, drink halfway to my mouth.

"Duke?" I swiveled on my bar stool. Sure enough, the tall, athletic build of the man standing before me belonged to my childhood best friend, Duke Ellis. Grinning, I placed my drink on the bar and stood, wrapping Duke in a tight embrace.

"Man, it's good to see you!" He hugged me back, bending to accommodate my shorter height.

"You too." I laughed, genuinely happy to see him. We'd started school together and had somehow managed to take every class together right up until graduation. I'd watched him turn from a tall, gangly teenager into a tall, muscular adult. His hair was pulled back into a ponytail, he sported a goatee beard and mustache, and his eyes still held that twinkle of mischief I remembered so well.

"What are you up to these days, Duke?" I asked, sitting back down and taking a sip of my beer. Sliding onto the bar stool next to me, Duke called out his order to the bartender before turning his attention to me.

"Oh, you know, a little bit of this, a little bit of that."

"Still smuggling, then?" I grinned. Duke drove a big rig and was happy to deliver anything to anybody, provided the price was right.

"Ah, now, Katie, let's not call it smuggling, eh? I'm an entrepreneur. I deliver what people want. I search out the most wanted items and provide them."

"At a price." I snorted.

"Of course." He grinned. Duke had always straddled the line of the law and, so far, had managed to keep his ass out of jail. "So, what brings you back to our fine town?" he asked.

"Work."

"Still with the cops?" It was ironic that when I'd lived in Maxxan, I'd been a deputy for the Maxxan Police Department, and my best friend was a crook.

"Kinda."

"One-word answers there, Shelton," he drawled, tossing some notes on the counter when the bartender delivered his drink.

"Need to know basis, Ellis."

He laughed. "And I don't need to know?"

"Exactly." I gave him a smile to soften the words. But Duke was used to me being tight-lipped about my job. Even when I was in the Police Force here, I never discussed work with him; this was nothing new.

"Ellis!" An overweight, middle-aged man came bustling through from the storeroom out back. "You got that order for me?"

"Sure do, Mack. One carton of red. It's in my truck; I'll get it. You got the cash?"

Mack glanced at me, clearly uncomfortable to be discussing business in front of me. "I'll come out," he said, flipping up the end of the bar, casting another suspicious glance my way before heading out the door.

"Watch my drink. I'll be back in a few." Duke slapped my shoulder a little too hard, then laughed as he walked away.

True to his word, he was back just a few minutes later, carrying a case of wine on one shoulder. He followed Mack behind the bar and into the storeroom before returning, tucking a wad of cash into the top pocket of his shirt.

"So, back to you, Katie. What are you doing drinking out here at Stanley's? There are nicer places in town." Duke grinned at me over the top of his beer bottle. Yeah, there were nicer bars in town, and that was where I'd been the night before. And picked up a stranger and had wickedly hot sex with him. It seemed prudent to avoid that bar for the moment.

"I like the ambiance here," I replied sarcastically, eyeballing the peeling paint and worn carpet.

"You were always such a bad liar." Duke chuckled. I studied him, and despite the fact we were both a few years older, he hadn't changed much.

"You ever do any work for Stillwater Pharmaceuticals?" I asked. It had occurred to me that he just might be in over his head with the very people I was hunting, given his occupation.

"Nah, I don't do drugs in any form. I'm more into antiquities and rare collectibles. Plus, they have a contract with a transport company, wouldn't even look at small fry like me."

I almost sagged in relief. It would have sucked if Duke had been involved.

"Is that why you're here? Because of those guys?"

"I can't talk about it, Duke. But please don't say anything, okay?" He studied me thoughtfully, then mimed the action of zipping his lips.

"Sorry I didn't make your grandma's funeral." I was grateful for the change of topic.

"That's okay. I only came back for the funeral and reading of the will," I replied, shrugging. I'd flown in that morning and out in the evening. I had no desire to spend any longer than necessary in Maxxan. How ironic that I was now leading the investigation into bringing Ridgeway and Byers to justice back in my hometown.

"That your first trip back, since you know, the…"

"The accident?" I cut him off. "Yes. First time."

"And you're okay now, Katie? After the *accident?*" He emphasized the word; I knew he did it to niggle at me, prod me to talk about what happened. I tightened my lips and ignored his subtle barb.

"Yes. I'm healed. I still have pain in my shoulder from time to time." I rotated my shoulder and felt the twinge from the damaged tendons and bone. The accident had been three years ago. I was as healed as I was going to get. Physically, that is. Emotionally, I wasn't sure I'd ever recover. Not completely. But I coped by burying myself in work, and like the counselors had told me, time helped. It didn't change anything, but it made the memories less sharp, less painful. But they were always there, just beneath the surface, and returning to Maxxan was making them difficult to ignore. The quicker we apprehended Ridgeway and Byers, the sooner I could get out of here and bury the past that haunted me.

FOUR

I spent a restless night at Rae's place, tossing and turning in one of the guest rooms, my memories threatening to drown me. At sunrise, I gave up any pretense of sleep and dressed in shorts, a tank, and running shoes. One thing I'd learned was that physical activity, pushing my body to breaking point, was a great distraction technique, and right now, I needed it. Badly.

Despite the early hour, it was already warm outside, but that didn't deter me. Fire demons love the heat; hence, my grandfather choosing Maxxan to settle down and raise a family. I headed out for my jog, my body falling into a familiar rhythm, my feet kicking up dust that soon stuck to my sweat-coated skin.

I ran for an hour. A blissful hour of nothing but my breath rasping in and out of my lungs, my hair dripping with sweat, my tank and shorts damp with it, but the endorphins pumping through my system lifted my mood. By the time I returned to the house, my head was clear.

Three work vehicles were parked in front of the house, and as I approached, I could read the name of a building contractor emblazoned on the side. Good. The work order I submitted had been approved, and we could set about turning the house into SIA offices.

"You Katie Shelton?" A middle-aged man with a big belly and flushed cheeks approached me with a sheet of crumpled paper in his hand. "Got a rush work order here that you want some work done?"

"Yeah," I puffed, coming to a halt and wiping the back of my arm across my forehead to stop the sweat dripping in my eyes. I didn't care that I must look a wreck—my appearance wasn't of any concern to anyone, least of all me. I took the sheet of paper from him and scanned it. This crew would take care of the construction inside. We'd combine the lounge room and dining room by knocking out the dividing wall and making one big workspace. The den would become executive offices, and

Grandma's bedroom would be an interrogation room.

"You have an electrician on your crew?" I asked, eyes sweeping over the motley gathering of men leaning against their respective vehicles, waiting for instructions.

"Two. Construction-wise, not too much to do, but your wiring needs updating, and I need to take a look at that...does that say 'cave'?" A stubby finger pointed to the paper I still held.

"It does. There's a cave beneath the house. We'll need a proper entrance secured; all doors need upgrading to reinforced steel. I've got the alarm people coming tomorrow—you understand you're getting paid above the usual rate to get this done fast?"

"Sure, that's why I brought extra crew." Snatching the paperwork from me, he crumpled it in his fist and shoved it into the back pocket of his coveralls. "Boys! Let's get to it. This is a rush job; it's gonna be a twelve-hour day." Groans met this news from their boss, and I bit back a grin. Twelve-hour shifts were the norm in the SIA; these men were soft.

I left them to do their walk-through of the house and turned my attention to the big rig truck rumbling down the drive, honking its air horn. I grinned. Trust Duke to land this job. Turning off the truck, the air brakes letting out a hiss, he jumped down from the cab.

"Morning, Miss Katie. Don't you look nice?" He grinned, tipping his baseball cap at me.

"Duke." I smiled, stepping forward to hug him.

"Ew gross. You're all sweaty!" He grimaced, shoving me away, while I laughed. "So. Renos at Grandma's house, eh?" He nodded toward the house, and I turned to look at it.

So many memories were within these walls, fun sleepovers with my cousins, sad times when Rae was locked away. I was the same age as Rae; I could relate better than anyone to what she went through.

"Yeah." I sighed, not too sure how I felt about the whole thing. All I knew was that it had been decided the SIA needed a permanent presence in Maxxan, that the town had somehow attracted the attention of the paranormal community and was now a beacon for criminal activity. While I was devoted to the SIA and bringing down Ridgeway and all of those involved in the illegal experiments, did it have to be in Maxxan, of all places?

Duke unfolded a sheet of paper from his top pocket. "So, I have instructions to clear out four bedrooms upstairs, the dining and living room, plus the den. Correct?"

"Yep, take it all."

"You got a few dollars to spend on replacing all that furniture, Katie?" he asked.

"Oh, come on, Duke, don't play dumb. It doesn't suit you," I chided. "You know this is SIA funded, that we're setting up shop here."

"Yeah, I do," he admitted, slinging an arm around my shoulders and looking at the house with me.

"I miss her," he said, referring to my grandma. I turned and looked up the hill to where two headstones sat beneath a tree.

"I do, too," I whispered, feeling my eyes well with tears. *Damn it all.* Blinking furiously, I wriggled away and wiped my arm across my eyes. "Let me show you what two rooms *not* to touch," I told him, heading down the front path of the house, leaving him to follow behind.

Rae and I had agreed to leave two of the upstairs bedrooms as-is for Rae or any family member to use should we need to. Currently, one room was Rae's, and I was using the other. There were six bedrooms upstairs, two of which would be converted into dorms with bunk beds for SIA staff, one would be turned into a medical bay, and the other for storage. In two days, Duke would be delivering a truckful of furniture and equipment to deck out the house and finalize its transition into SIA offices.

It was chaos inside. The work crew had split into groups and were examining their respective work areas, bitching about the furniture being in the way. Tape measures were whipped out; someone had set up a transistor radio, and music interspersed with static fought for dominance over their voices. After giving Duke a tour and watching as he flagged everything that was to be removed with an orange sticker, I retreated to the kitchen for a much-needed coffee. Downstairs, the kitchen and laundry were the only rooms that would be untouched.

I was waiting by the machine, staring at the tiles, and thinking of nothing when I felt it. A pressure change in the atmosphere. Turning my head, I peered over my shoulder, mouth dropping open when the man I'd been avoiding even thinking about, the stranger I'd slept with, stood in the doorway, arms crossed over his chest.

"What the hell?"

"We meet again." His eyes ran the length of me, from the top of my head to the tip of my toes, and I became painfully aware of my sweaty, dusty appearance. Me? Who didn't give a damn about what anyone thought, gave a damn what this man thought? *What was up with that?*

"Are you from the satellite company?" I asked, narrowing my eyes. I'd arranged for a satellite to be installed so we could network with SIA HQ in Redmeadows.

"Nope." He shook his head.

"Security?" I tried. Along with perimeter alarms and cameras, keypad locks would be installed on all doors inside and outside the house.

"Nope." One corner of his mouth curled into a smirk, and I knew he was enjoying this. He reached into the back pocket of his jeans, pulled out a wallet, flipped it open, and presented it to me. Inside was a badge. Oh, no. Tell me it wasn't true. I leaned forward to read it.

"Secret Service?" *They'd sent the Secret Service on an SIA case?*

"Agent Brax Lane. And you are SIA Katie Shelton." He flipped his wallet closed and shoved it back in his pocket, seeming incredibly pleased with himself.

"You knew who I was?" I demanded, my hackles rising

But he was already shaking his head. "No,

ma'am, I did not. Not until I got my orders this morning."

I stared at him in stunned disbelief, digesting what he'd said. Then the coffee machine beeped, and I turned my attention to it, pouring myself a cup of the strong black brew. I needed it more than ever.

"Mind if I?" he asked, reaching above me to grab a cup down from the shelf. I shrugged and moved out of his way.

Cradling the steaming brew in my hands, I hustled down the hallway and out onto the back deck. *This could not be happening.* He was a one-night stand. A stranger I had no intention of seeing again. Ever. How could he be here? In my house? Correction, I told myself, in SIA Offices declaring he was Secret Service? I hadn't been notified we'd be working with them. Pulling out my phone, I dialed.

"Nate—tell me you didn't send Secret Service down here," I demanded when my boss answered.

"No choice, Katie," Nate replied before he muffled the phone, and I heard him say in the background, "*Yes, it's Katie. No, call her in your own time; she's working. Yes, I'll say hello to her.*"

To me, he said, "Paige says hello."

"Whatever," I grumbled, annoyed beyond belief.

"The Secret Service is investigating my chopper

getting shot down," Nate told me, "and given what happened at Stillwater Pharmaceuticals, they requested to assist in our investigation. Which is a polite way of saying they are joining in, like it or not."

"You could have warned me."

"I found out literally ten minutes ago. I take it an agent has turned up?" There was amusement in Nate's voice, and it just fueled my irritability.

"Yes. Only he's been in Maxxan for a couple of days. So, they were planning this before they notified you."

"I'm not surprised."

"How can you not give a shit?" My voice rose. "This is our investigation, Nate. Now the Secret Service wants to swoop in and take all the credit."

Nate blew out a breath. "The more people on this, the quicker Ridgeway is caught and stopped. I'd think you'd want that, Katie, to keep your family safe?"

He had me. *Damn it all to hell.*

"Fine." I huffed, disconnecting the call and sliding my phone back into the pocket of my shorts.

The screen door slapped against its frame, and I glanced over to see Duke, coffee cup in hand, heading my way.

"Slacking off already?" Despite everything, I was still happy to see my best friend.

"Refueling." He raised his cup and clinked it with mine. "What's up? You look pissed."

"Work stuff." I breathed out a heavy sigh. I had no control over working with Brax Lane, but I needed to make one thing clear to him—there would be no repeat of the other night. No matter what the sight of him in his butt-hugging jeans and black T-shirt that molded to his chest and clung to his abs in just the right way did to my insides. He was an itch that I would not scratch. No way. Wasn't going to happen.

"Didn't you say this wasn't going to happen again?" Brax rolled to his side, taking me with him. We were both breathless; our bodies sheened with sweat, and in the air the lingering scent of sex

"It wasn't. It isn't." I wriggled away from his embrace to sit on the edge of the bed, shaking my head at my weakness. It had been a long day, I told myself, and all day he'd been burrowing under my defenses, being *nice*. Charming even. And all day, I'd been hyper-aware of him—every time I was within two feet of him, the hairs on my arms stood up, my heart beat a little faster, and my lady bits went into overdrive.

My family had turned up to undergo training, as instructed. I'd started them off, and then Brax had taken over, freeing me up to oversee the work on the house.

Now it was late; the workmen had left; the house was empty...it was just the two of us. Outside, thunder rumbled in the distance. A storm was rolling in, matching my mood perfectly, for I was a jumble of emotions. Besides lust, want, and desire, were also guilt, remorse, and regret.

"Katie." He heard it in my voice. All of it. The weight of my name on his lips spoke volumes.

"I'm sorry. I didn't intend for that to happen. It's on me. It won't happen again." I pulled on my clothes, refusing to make eye contact. That's what had been my undoing in the first place, looking into those melted chocolate eyes, watching them darken into swirling pools of desire. I'd stepped up to him, chest to chest, and kissed him. He'd kissed me back. And here we were, rolling in the sheets in my bedroom.

Snatching up my shoes, I fled, rushing downstairs and out the front door. I needed to put as much distance between us as I could, which meant I had to leave. Temporarily, at least. Enough time for him to dress and clear out.

The air outside was hot and thick with the promise of the impending storm. Forks of lightning could be seen in the distance, adding a flair of drama to my hasty retreat. Sitting on the step, I pulled on my shoes, berating myself for what had just happened. What was I thinking? Why did I lose control around him? There were no rules to say we couldn't fraternize; there was nothing to stop us except for my sense of what was right and what I considered professional behavior. This wasn't it.

Hearing a floorboard creak inside spurred me into action. No doubt he wanted to talk, to discuss *us*, but he failed to understand that there was no us. We had chemistry, sure. But that was it. Nothing more.

Pushing to my feet, I ran down the front path to my truck. I'd driven to Maxxan from Redmeadows, despite Nate's offer of a plane ticket and hire car. I liked driving, and it had been a long time since I'd been on the open highway, nothing but miles of road ahead of me.

I drove mindlessly for over an hour. It wasn't until the flashes of lightning became so frequent and blinding that I pulled over and decided I'd sit out the storm in the cab of my truck that I realized where I was. Had I intended to come here all along?

Opening the truck door, I dropped to the ground and stood in the street, looking at the house I'd parked in front of. Around me, the storm raged. The wind picked up, buffeting me, but I braced my legs against it and stood as the rain started to fall in big heavy drops, soaking me to the skin within seconds.

All I saw was the house. *Our house*. Memories overlaid reality, and I saw it as it was then. The sun shining, another hot day in Maxxan. The front door opened, and Ethan came out, smiling and talking over his shoulder, the light catching his blonde hair, making it shimmer. I followed behind him, Abigail balanced on my hip, her tiny fingers tangled in my hair—it was long then, reaching past my shoulders—tugging and pulling and laughing at my exaggerated winces. I handed her to Ethan to secure in her car seat while I slid behind the wheel, waiting for Ethan to finish and join me. Putting the car into reverse, I backed out of the driveway, moved the car into drive, and headed off down the street.

I stood now in the pouring rain, watching as the phantom car's taillights disappeared into nothing. Nothing but ghosts of the past. That was our last day. A shuddering breath tore through my chest. Then another, and another. Tears fell thick and fast, mingling with the rain, compounding with the crippling pain in my chest. I dropped to my knees, my world collapsing around me, my arms aching to hold my little girl once more, to smell the precious scent of her skin, to see her cherub lips curl into a smile, to listen to her babble nonsense to her momma.

I sobbed, my heart cracked wide open in my chest, and I feared it would never heal, for the pain today felt as raw and real as it had three years ago, the day they died.

Eventually, the storm overhead began to clear, as did the storm within me. My tears slowed, and I staggered to my feet, shaky beyond belief at the emotional battering. I climbed into my truck, locked the door, and lay across the front seat, curling into a ball. I was done. Spent. I had nothing left in me, was nothing but a shell. Closing my eyes, I slept.

"Jesus, you look rough." Duke's mouth hung open, and I scowled at him, perfectly aware of my bloodshot, puffy eyes, complete with dark shadows.

"Thanks," I snapped. The emotional storm of

last night may have been cleansing, may have been long overdue, but the physical aftereffects lingered. For one, I was exhausted, and two, as Duke had said, I looked a wreck. Not to mention my short temper. I'd been snapping at the workmen all day, driving them hard to get the house finished. Brax had cleared out, no doubt not wanting to be on the receiving end of anything I had to dish out today. I knew my mood was foul. Hell, I couldn't stand to be around myself, so I couldn't blame him. And that made my mood even worse.

Eventually, I'd climbed into my truck and driven into town, pulling to a stop in the parking lot of Stanley's.

"Rough day?" A shot glass appeared in front of me, and I slammed it down. The alcohol burned, but I didn't cough, just blinked a few times before focusing on the bartender and signaling for another.

"You could say that." I played with the empty shot glass and looked at Duke, who'd seated himself on the bar stool next to me. My best friend. And I suddenly realized how much I'd missed him. Three years was a long time.

"Sorry I didn't keep in touch," I said now, lowering my eyes to the shot glass as I spun it around in my fingers.

Silence greeted my words, then a hard pat on my back, so hard I almost face-planted into the bar, and Duke said, "It's okay, Shelton. I get it." Which was code for we don't need to talk about it.

And the shots kept coming. Someone dropped a quarter in the jukebox, and country tunes began blaring.

"Seriously? Stanley needs to update his collection."

"You know Stanley doesn't actually own Stanley's anymore?" Duke replied.

"Get outta town! No fucking way! I thought he'd die here."

"Seems he got an offer he couldn't refuse."

I squinted, studying Duke. "You bought it, didn't you? Son of a bitch, Duke Ellis, you bought this bar!"

"Shhh, keep your voice down. The whole town doesn't need to know," he grumbled, head swiveling to see if anyone overheard.

"Why not?"

"I have a reputation to uphold."

"Pft, what? Unlawful smuggler? I know how you hate being one of the good guys, Duke," I laughed. *Hilarious.*

"Just don't tell anyone, okay?" I watched as his eyes followed the path of a young woman walking across the room. He was already halfway off the bar stool and heading in her direction. Yeah. He hadn't changed. Duke liked everyone to think he was a bad guy, but deep down, he wasn't.

Someone took his place on the barstool next to me; I could feel their stare. I waited a couple of minutes, but their manners didn't kick in, so I turned and scowled.

"If you're going to stare that hard, you should at least introduce yourself."

He was an okay-looking guy, average in every way. My heart didn't skip a beat; my skin didn't tingle. Nor did anything else. But by the way his eyes raked over me, the disinterest wasn't mutual. I sighed.

"Bartender! Get the lady another one of whatever she's drinking."

Oh good. Free drinks. And an asshole who thought I'd owe him.

"I'll take the drink, but let me be clear. Not. Interested."

He barked out a laugh. "You can't blame a man for trying."

"You expect to pick up in a place that smells like bad beer and worse choices?" I slammed down the shot and grinned. "It's working—I'm all boozy inside." My words were coated in heavy sarcasm, and he laughed again.

"I like you." He was still chuckling, shaking his head.

"Wait until you get to know the real me," I told him. "I'm a total bitch. Seriously. Run now while you still can, before I chew you up and spit you out, broken in places you never knew could be broken."

"I love a challenge." He moved closer until our shoulders were touching.

"Ew. Dude. No. Just no." I slid off my barstool, balanced my hand on the bar, and waited while the room righted itself. "I already told you, not interested, not going to happen."

He reached out a hand to touch my face, and I grabbed it, twisting his arm up behind his back and slamming his face into the bar. "I. Said. No." I growled in his ear. "You think buying me a drink entitles you to anything? I'll give you one shot, right between the eyes."

"Hey, hey, hey." Duke appeared, resting his hand gently on my shoulder. "You bothering this lady?" He addressed the man, who was groaning in agony, his face squashed into the bar.

"No," he choked out.

"Okay then." Duke nodded, then squeezed my

shoulder. "Let him go, Katie." I looked at Duke, then released my grip, and the man jumped away, cradling his arm against his chest. His mouth opened to release a tirade, but Duke held up a hand. "I wouldn't if I were you. I suggest you leave before the lady changes her mind and puts a shot right between your baby blues. And I can attest to the fact that she's a damn fine shot."

Of course, I wasn't going to shoot the man, but I laughed anyway. The man took one last look at me, decided I was crazy, and fled.

"I was handling it," I grumbled as the room dipped and swayed.

Duke peered into my eyes and shook his head. "Shelton, you're wasted."

"I do believe I am." I blinked, only I couldn't seem to get my eyes open again. Damn stupid eyelids. Duke blew out a breath, and then I was being scooped up and tossed over his shoulder.

"Come on. And you'd better not puke," he muttered.

"No promises." The movement made my stomach churn, yet I still couldn't seem to open my eyes and see where we were going. I heard a door slam, felt the night air on my face, and dragged in a deep, refreshing breath. Then we were climbing upstairs. Another door. The click of a switch; then I was being lowered none too gently.

"Sleep it off," he said. Then the light was switched off, and I was surrounded by darkness. So, I slept.

CHAPTER
SIX

"Let me tell you how Maxxan works. Everyone pretends the whole town isn't overrun with paranormals," Sheriff Kevin Brady barked. We were in his office, the door closed. It was time for *that* conversation. The one where local law enforcement was brought up to speed on the SIA—and Secret Service since Agent Brax Lane was sitting next to me, dressed again in black jeans and a black T-shirt, and looking so damn fucking delicious it was amazing I didn't slide clean off my chair.

"The majority of the population are unaware," I said. The sheriff's belligerence was coming at me in waves. He didn't like us, didn't like that we were on his turf, doing what he considered to be his job.

"Who will keep the drunks off the road? Who will keep the ordinary, everyday, non-paranormal citizens of Maxxan safe? Just be a good cop. It matters." I tried to reassure him.

Of course, the sheriff knew about paranormals. Agent Buchanan had filled him in during his time in Maxxan, but that had been on a need-to-know basis–he was given the bare minimum. But now, the SIA was here to stay, and we needed to work hand in hand with local law enforcement. I hoped it would help that I'd been a deputy here just a few short years ago. It seemed the sheriff remembered that very thing, for he sat back slowly in his chair and nodded.

"Working out of the old Shelton property, you say?"

"Yeah." I nodded. "We have the property at our disposal, and it's out of the way. We won't disturb the townsfolk out there."

"And you?" He addressed Brax. "You're from the Secret Service, you say?"

"Only here to get the job done, and then I'll be out of your hair," Brax told him. We'd filled the sheriff in on the latest threat, what we thought was going on at Stillwater Pharmaceuticals. We needed his help to get a search warrant. We were going in strong, and we were going in legally. Nate and Paige had already broken into the facility once. There was a strong possibility that anything incriminating was already cleared out. Still, on the off chance they were cocky enough not to move the drug they were using to experiment on paranormals, we needed full access. We needed to go deep, forensically deep on their records, uncover every little thing they'd been hiding. The only way to get it was with a search warrant.

"Very well. I'll put in for a warrant. But my boys will be with you on the search."

"Agreed." Brax rose and shook the sheriff's hand. I followed suit.

"Good to have you back, Shelton. You've been missed."

"Thank you."

Brax followed me out of the station. "This is your old workplace, huh? Before SIA?"

"Don't play dumb," I grumbled. "You've read my file. You know my history."

But he surprised me by shaking his head. "I know you're SIA, Katie. I don't know how you got there. But I saw your photo on the wall of the station in a deputy's uniform. Put two and two together. Why did you leave here?"

"Is that the time?" Glancing at my watch, I headed off, not answering him. I wanted to get back and check on the progress of the construction crew; they were scheduled to finish today. The SIA had paid an astronomical amount of cash to get the work done to our timeframes, and a job that would have taken weeks to complete was done in days. Money talks.

Plus, I had the satellite company arriving to install the dish and network the computers that should be waiting. I'd received a text to say they'd been delivered, and after waking up on Duke's sofa this morning, I'd yet to return to make sure everything was on track.

"You didn't come back." Brax caught up, and I bit back a curse. I did not want to talk about it. At all. Ever.

"Nope."

"I waited."

"Didn't ask you to." In fact, that had been the very reason I'd left. I wanted him gone because the temptation was almost too difficult to resist when he was near. Why did my body respond to him this way? It was like as soon as he was within a certain radius, my hormones went crazy, haywire, and all I could think about was jumping his bones. Even now, my mind was flashing images of his naked flesh, and I swiped at my lip in case I inadvertently drooled at the memory.

"Look, we both know the other night shouldn't have happened. The fact that it did is on me. My bad." I kept walking, forgetting my truck that was parked in front of the sheriff's office. It wasn't until I was at the corner, considering which direction to turn, that I realized I'd walked right past it.

"I'm not complaining." I knew Brax had a wicked grin from ear to ear without even looking. I could hear it in his voice, the sexy dip at the end.

"It's not happening again." Spinning on my heel, I backtracked, legs eating up the sidewalk at a rapid pace. I had to focus on the job at hand. Then Brax would be gone, and this irritating attraction would go with it.

"Sure about that? Because I'm pretty sure I've heard those words from you before."

"Look." I stopped and jabbed him in the chest with a finger. "I'm here to do a job. So are you. I suggest we both concentrate on the task at hand. I'm not interested in sleeping with you again, and I'd appreciate it if you'd stop bringing it up."

"What are you running from, Katie?" He wrapped his fingers around my hand to stop me from poking him again, and the contact sent a bolt of lightning up my arm.

"Nothing. And don't touch me." Snatching my hand back, I stalked to my truck and climbed inside, slamming the door. He sidled up to the open window, leaned his arm against the roof, and studied me intently.

"You've made your position clear," he said, voice somber, "but now it's my turn. Believe it or not, I like you, Katie Shelton. A lot. And I want to get to know you a whole lot better. So, no, I'm not backing off, going away, leaving you alone. We have a connection, you and I, one I've never experienced before, and I intend to explore what that's all about fully."

My heart stopped. It literally stopped beating in my chest, and I stared at him in horror, hand flattening against my chest.

"Katie?" He straightened, concern evident on his face. "Breathe. Just breathe."

Breathe? Was he insane? I was having a heart attack, I was dying, and he wanted me to breathe? The truck door was wrenched open, and he swiveled me sideways, shoving my head down between my knees and leaning between my shoulder blades when I struggled to get back up.

"Heart attack!" I sputtered, dragging in a breath despite myself.

"It's not a heart attack. It's a panic attack. You're okay; you're not dying."

"I'm not?" I squeaked.

"No." A few more seconds passed, with me gulping in big gulps of air and him leaning a massive hand on my back, preventing me from sitting up. Until I came to my senses, and heat burned my cheeks.

"I'm okay. Let me up," I said. He released me and stepped back. I sat up, brushed the hair from my face, and slammed shut the truck door. Without a word, I turned the key in the ignition and drove away. I would have to expand that little box in my head that was stuffed with memories I didn't want to see the light of day. Having a panic attack in front of Brax Lane—hell, pretty much every memory involving Brax Lane had to go in there. Then I'd close the lid and lock it down. Tight.

"WHO DO I have to sleep with to get a drink around here?" The familiar drawl of my cousin Rae had me looking up from the laptop I was currently working on.

"Rae! You're here!" Coming around my newly set up workstation, I hugged her.

"Of course. Think I'd let you take all the credit?" Rae laughed, then cupped my shoulders, peering into my face. "How are you holding up?"

I couldn't hold her stare, so I focused my attention on the wall over her shoulder. "Oh, you know. Okay."

"Bullshit." She laughed again, but let go of me with a slap on the arm. "You know my lie detector is better than anyone's. But I'll let it slide this time."

"Where's Jordan?" I changed the subject. I still wasn't ready to talk about Ethan and Abigail. Doubt I ever would be.

"Bringing in the bags." I heard the front door open, and Rae leaned her head out into the hallway. "Upstairs to the left."

"I remember." Jordan appeared in the doorway. "Hi, Katie. Looks good in here." He nodded to the workstations that were now set up with computers fully networked to SIA HQ in Redmeadows. We were good to go. The technician was currently working on installing keyless locks on the doors, and we were done.

"It still feels strange to me," I admitted, glancing around the room that had once been our living and dining rooms. "Thanks for coming," I told them both, grateful not only for the help they would bring to the investigation but also for the buffer of people I could put between Brax and me. The more, the better.

"Turns out this Ridgeway chick has been a thorn in the SIA's side for quite some time, so I'm all in on bringing the bitch down." Rae nodded, planting her hands on her hips. "So where are we at?"

"Actually, that's perfect timing." I hadn't heard Brax come in, and it seemed neither did Rae, for she jumped when he spoke behind her.

"Fuck!" she gasped, hand to her chest. "If you sneak around like that all the time, I'm gonna put a bell on you."

"Apologies, ma'am." Brax held out a hand. "Secret Service Agent Brax Lane. And you must be Rae Shelton."

Rae shook his hand and gave him the once over. "I heard the Secret Service elbowed in on our case." She softened the words with a grin, which widened considerably when Jordan came back downstairs and joined us. More introductions followed before Rae brought us back to the case in hand. "You said perfect timing. When you came in and scared the shit out of me," she elaborated at Jordan's puzzled look. "Perfect timing for what?"

"Sheriff Brady has the warrant. We're to meet him at Stillwater Pharmaceuticals in one hour. Suit up; this one is official."

"The sheriff called you?" I bristled. This was our investigation; I was leading it; it should have been me he'd called. I made a mental note to have a word with the sheriff and make sure he understood the lay of the land.

"Something wrong with that?" Brax asked. Rae looked from Brax to me and back again, not missing a thing.

"I'm going to change into uniform. I'll be back in five," she said, hurrying upstairs with Jordan right behind her. They'd arrived in civilian clothing, but since this was an official search, what Brax had said was right—we needed to suit up in official SIA gear.

"Same." I hurried upstairs to my room and pulled on the black uniform specially designed to withstand sharp claws. I'd opted not to wear the black yoga-style pants, instead going for the cargo pants—the extra pockets came in handy. Black tank, followed by a tight-fitting zip-up jacket that, when done up, covered my throat. The sleeves had thumb loops to protect my wrists. Around my waist, I slung my belt, slid my pyre gun into its holster, and clipped on my red SIA badge. Boots were next, knee high with space inside for blades, and then the black baseball cap with the SIA emblem embroidered in red.

I beat Rae by mere seconds, grinning at her in triumph. We'd always been competitive as children, and nothing had changed since becoming adults. Now that Rae was with the SIA, she'd made it her mission to climb the ranks as quickly as possible— she had her sights set on becoming an Enforcer like me.

"Looking good, Guardian." I grinned at her, admiring the gleam of her long brown curls pulled into a ponytail through the back of her cap. My hair had been that long. Once. With a quick shake of my head, I glanced around for Brax. Where had he gone? I'd no quicker thought it than I heard it. A low, threatening growl.

"Bear's here?" I smiled in delight, flinging open the front door to find Bear stalking Brax, who had his hands up and was ever so slowly edging backward, muttering, "easy, easy" as he went.

"It's okay, Bear; he's with us." Rae whistled, and the giant hellhound turned his big head toward her.

Then he spotted me. His tongue flopped out, and his tail wagged, and he bounded over to drop at my feet for a pat.

"Hey, boy! I've missed you." Even lying on the ground, he came up to my shoulders, and I did my best to wrap my arms around his neck and hug him. Bear had been summoned to earth by some vampires and had taken a liking to Rae and had decided he'd become her pet; they'd been inseparable ever since.

"That's a...hellhound." Brax sounded like he was in shock. "How can I even see it? And what's it doing here?"

"Bear belongs to Rae; he adopted her when she came home last time. And yeah, while hellhounds are usually incorporeal, we discovered that if you're connected to Rae, you can see him."

"Right. Of course," he muttered, running a hand around the back of his neck and regrouping. "I was going to suggest we all go in my vehicle, but there's no way he's going to fit."

"That's okay; we brought our truck for that very reason." Rae pointed to their pickup with the large tray on the back. "Up," she instructed Bear, who obediently stepped into the back, lying down with his chin resting on the cabin.

"Looks like it's just you and me," Brax said to me. I ignored him and stalked to the vehicle.

The drive to Stillwater Pharmaceuticals was spent in silence. Several times Brax opened his mouth and turned toward me, a question on his lips, but then he'd reconsider and shut his mouth and face forward again. I assumed he was still getting his head around the fact my cousin has a pet hellhound.

After clearing security at the gate, we pulled into the parking lot. Sheriff Brady was already here, leaning against his patrol car. By his side, Deputy Chase Harvey. I was surprised to see Chase. Last I knew, he was working on a mine five hundred miles away.

"Sheriff. Deputy." I climbed out of Brax's car and nodded at the law enforcement officers.

"Wowee, Katie Shelton, you look hawt," Chase drawled, eyes crawling over me. "That's some uniform. Why can't we have uniforms like that instead of this god-awful beige?" he complained to the Sheriff.

"Focus on the job at hand, Harvey." The Sheriff sighed, and I bit back a grin.

"Between us, we have three teams," Brax said, cutting across the chitchat, an edge of steel to his voice. "Sheriff, you and the deputy focus on the administrative offices. Me and Shelton will take the labs, and Buchanan and the other Shelton will take the warehouse."

"Sounds good to me." Straightening up, the sheriff slapped the search warrant against his thigh. "Let's get this over with."

"Stop telling me—and everyone else—what to do," I hissed at Brax, dropping back a couple of feet so the sheriff couldn't hear us as we followed him across the parking lot to the reception area.

"What? I'm just doing my job," he said defensively, and I shot him an angry look.

"This is my investigation. I'm the lead. I don't need you to tell me how to do it." I didn't give him the chance to reply, stalking ahead and stepping in behind the sheriff as he opened the door.

CHAPTER

SEVEN

We didn't find anything of consequence at Stillwater Pharmaceuticals, but then I hadn't expected to. They'd have realized their operation was compromised as soon as Nate and Paige had broken in. Still, it was the only lead we had at this stage, and I could only hope the forensic searching of their digital data would turn up something, some small thread we could pull and follow.

Of course, that would take time. We'd linked their hard drives to our IT department in Redmeadows before heading back to our new SIA offices. Now we had to wait while they scoured the databases, and God only knows how long that would take.

"Sleep well?" Rae beamed at me the following morning as she sat down at the workstation opposite.

"No. I did not," I grumbled, then kicked myself for the frown that darkened Rae's face.

"What's wrong?" She was instantly concerned, and while I loved my cousin dearly, this was one of the reasons I'd joined the SIA. To get away from my overly concerned family.

"What's wrong is that I had the dubious pleasure of listening to you and Jordan having sex half the night."

A sly grin replaced the frown, and Rae leaned back in her chair. "Oh," was all she said.

"Yeah, *oh*, indeed." All I'd had was about three hours of sleep. Which meant Jordan and Rae should be sleep-deprived too, but here they both were, bright-eyed and full of pep. I wanted to bang their heads together.

"What's the plan today?" Jordan asked, and my irritation fled in an instant. He'd turned to me for orders. He and I were both Enforcers, both at the same level, yet Nate had entrusted me to lead this case, and Jordan was respectful of that.

"Paige told us that her friend, Lani's mom, was a ghoul. That was the connection at the time between Stillwater Pharmaceuticals and the ghoul population. You and Rae pay her a visit. See what you can find." I paused, tapping my finger against my lips. "Can Bear scent ghouls?"

"We're going to find out." Rae was all business, and her energy was infectious. The SIA clearly agreed with her, and I was glad, for she'd had such a bad deal of it throughout her youth, being admitted to a psychiatric facility when she was eighteen and labeled insane when she wasn't. Life hadn't treated her fairly, yet here she was, healed, whole, and well-adjusted. I'd been through nothing like what she'd suffered, yet I remained broken.

I knew it but wouldn't admit it, not to anyone, that my ability to love was gone. It had died along with my fiancé and daughter. As they bled out in the mangled wreck of our car on the highway, I'd prayed that I would die with them, that I wouldn't be forced to endure the torture of living without the two people I loved most in the world. Fate had other ideas. I survived. They did not. My heart kept beating, and I kept living, but inside I was dead, incapable of loving again.

After seeing Rae and Jordan off, I returned to my

desk. The door keypads were being fitted this morning. Someone needed to be onsite to receive the pass cards, and instructions on resetting them and issuing new ones should the need arise. While the locksmith was doing that, I hacked into the sheriff's database and ran a search for missing persons. Maxxan had plenty of secrets, and I had a hunch more was going on here than what we already knew about.

I was in the kitchen on my seventh or was that eighth cup of coffee for the day when Brax arrived. Of course, he couldn't get in because the front door was now locked, and he didn't have a keycard. Holding my coffee in hand, I made my way to the front door where Brax was currently pounding and calling my name.

"Okay, okay, I'm here, geez," I smirked, knowing he could hear me but not see me since I hadn't opened the door yet.

"Katie? Let me in," he demanded. I paused, considering. This was my turf. This was SIA, and I was in charge of SIA in Maxxan—for now, at least.

"Okay, okay, I get it. You're the boss. I'll stop giving you orders. Just open the door. Please." Damn it; he'd spoiled my fun way too early. With a huff, I pressed the button by the door, and it clicked open.

"Thank you," he said with exaggerated politeness. I shrugged and returned to my workstation.

"Would it be okay if I set up here? Naturally, I won't use the SIA Servers, and I have my own laptop, but it makes sense for us to pool our information, and it's easier if we're in one location."

"Fair enough," I replied, watching my screen as the search I'd run trolled through the database.

He chose a workstation to my right, and I watched out of the corner of my eye as he opened his laptop and was soon engrossed with whatever was on his screen.

"Can I ask you something?" he asked.

"You just did."

"Haha. So, this place,"—he waved a hand around—"you're heading the Maxxan office of the SIA?"

"I'm running this current investigation. Once we have Ridgeway, I'll be returning to Redmeadows. Why?"

"No reason. Just curious."

He was silent for a while, making me jump when he suddenly said, "I've got something!"

"There's a cream for that," I joked.

"You're full of sass today." He smiled, leaning back in his chair, arms crossed over his chest.

"What did you find?" I asked, not liking the way he was looking at me. Like he imagined me with no clothes on. Unfortunately, as soon as that thought entered my head, all I could see was him—naked. A rush flooded my body, and I cursed my hormones.

"That there has been a lot of death by animal attacks in Maxxan lately," he said.

"That was going to be my next search." I sighed. He'd beaten me to the punch. Again.

"Why? What are you working on?"

"Missing persons. That's been Ridgeway's MO in the past. Snatch humans off the street to experiment on, preferably ones who wouldn't be easily missed, wouldn't be reported."

"Good call."

"Why, thank you," I replied sarcastically.

Brax stood and left the room, and I watched his retreating back in surprise. Shaking my head, I returned my attention to my screen. There were a handful of missing persons, and my eyes zeroed in on one name in particular. Mrs. B. Lani had reported her missing a week ago, just before I'd returned to Maxxan. Pulling out my mobile, I phoned Jordan.

"Mrs. B was reported missing by her daughter a week ago," I said as soon as he answered.

"Yeah, we figured she was gone. Her place is empty, mailbox overflowing, indoor plants wilting, food in the fridge is starting to turn."

"Did Bear pick up anything?"

"Rae is out with him now. It looks like he did pick up a scent, but whether it will lead us to anything, we don't know. I'll catch up with her as soon as I've finished here. I want to be thorough, see if she slipped up and left any clue as to where she might have been headed, what her next steps are."

"Keep me posted. And keep an eye on Rae. She's new at this." I was nervous that he'd left her to follow Mrs. B's trail alone. Although she did have Bear with her, and he was a formidable opponent who would fight tooth and nail to protect her.

"Will do." He hung up, and I slowly did the same, startled when I noticed Brax by my side, my coffee cup in his hand.

"Hey, that's mine!" I reached for it, and he handed it over.

"Decaf," he said, returning to his seat. "You're all jittery. I think you've had enough caffeine for one day."

"Don't tell me what to do," I grumbled.

"Do you want to hear about these animal attacks or not?"

Taking a sip of my coffee, I eyeballed him over the rim of my cup. "Yes."

"It looks like Maxxan has always had its fair share of animal attacks over the years," he began. When I opened my mouth to interrupt, he held up his hand. "Let me finish." I shut my mouth with a snap. "Go ahead."

"Some of them are most likely legitimate. After all, Maxxan is surrounded by wilderness. There are coyotes and all sorts of creatures out there capable of killing a human. I can see certain fluctuations, though, especially over the past five years, like clusters of attacks."

This caught my attention, and I rose to peer over his shoulder at his screen. He'd mapped out the attacks on a timeline. He was right. There were spikes. Starting five years ago, with four spikes, but slowly diminishing to two spikes a year.

"Could this be related to the vampires and their drug crops, though? Maybe at harvest time, there were more vampires in town, meaning more deaths."

"Could be. I'm going to pull autopsy reports— it'll take a while."

"I'll help. Send me a list of names."

"I'm looking for types of injuries. Where on the body, that type of thing." Then he realized what he'd said. "Sorry. I know you know what to look for. I wasn't telling you how to do your job."

"I know." I shrugged and turned my attention to my monitor, where his email had just arrived. He'd given me half the list. Just over one hundred names. It was staggering to realize that two hundred people had died from animal attacks over the last five years. Why hadn't people moved away? Or were they oblivious?

"I'd like to track the background info on the victims, too," I said. "Like, did they have family here? Would they be missed? Or not."

"You think it's connected?"

"Maybe." I shrugged, "Maybe not. But that's a hell of a lot of people to die and not have the world pay any attention to it. It's like it's all gone under the radar."

"A cover-up?"

"Most likely. Let's see what we can find. I want to know if any of these could be linked to ghouls."

"Ghouls usually take possession of a body," he pointed out.

"Not always. And if they need food, they make a

kill. I want to know if body parts were missing that were never retrieved."

The hours passed, each of us engrossed in our research. Behind me, where Grandma's television used to sit, was now an electronic case board. Whenever an autopsy result came up that looked of interest, I'd flick it to the board. Brax did the same. Soon, we had a collection of suspicious animal deaths that could have been a result of a paranormal attack for all intents and purposes. Or experiments by Ridgeway. I still wasn't sure if she was the link, not in all of these cases. Still, the SIA intended to have a permanent presence in Maxxan, which meant digging into the cover-ups by local law enforcement.

I was in the middle of reading a particularly gruesome autopsy report on a young man who had been disemboweled when my phone buzzed.

"You need to get here." Jordan's voice came through as soon as I hit connect.

"What's happened?" I was already on my feet. I tossed a pass card at Brax as I rounded my desk and headed to the front door.

"Rae needs you." A shiver ran down my spine.

"What's happened, Buchanan?" I snapped, needing answers.

"We found her. Mrs. B."

"And?" By now, I was out the front door and hurrying to my truck, Brax hot on my heels.

"Dead. A shallow grave."

"Where?"

I followed Jordan's directions to a small patch of parkland not far from Mrs. B's house. It was getting late in the day, the sun close to dipping below the horizon—we'd lose light soon. I jogged across the park to where I could see Jordan standing with his arm around Rae's shoulders. Bear lay by her side.

"You okay?" I addressed Rae, who was a lovely shade of gray.

She nodded. "Sorry. I puked on the crime scene."

"It happens. This your first?"

She shook her head. "No, I saw a vampire kill back when Jordan first came to Maxxan when we were searching for the gunslinger. But this one? This is so...gross." She pointed, and I turned, seeing a shallow grave a few feet away.

"You dug it out?" I asked Jordan, approaching the grave. The smell was the first thing that hit me, that undeniable stench of rotting flesh.

"Nope. Found it like this. Think they may have been disturbed, so they fled, left it like this."

Like this was a body that had been torn apart.

Both arms had been wrenched from the torso and chewed on. Chunks of flesh were missing. The torso and abdomen were ripped open, and I'd guess most, if not all, of her internal organs were gone. The once sparkling eyes of Mrs. B were now wide open, glazed over with a film of white. I reminded myself that the real Mrs. B had died a long time ago, that the ghoul had taken over her body. And now he'd discarded it. Probably because he knew he was busted, that we were on to him.

Pulling out my phone, I dialed the sheriff. Mrs. B was on the missing person list, and Lani deserved closure.

"Sheriff's on his way. Jordan, take Rae back home. Rae, you need to write this up. I want a report on my desk before you sign off for the night."

"Got it," Rae replied with a nod.

"Oh, here. Take these, or you won't get in." I tossed two pass cards at them, remembering home wasn't really home anymore. It was the Maxxan branch of the SIA.

After they'd left, I examined the scene. The body had been here for a couple of days at least, possibly more, but due to the heat, decomposition was fast. I couldn't guess the time of death. Not that it was important. The ghoul who'd inhabited her body had bailed, and judging from the mess he'd made, more than one ghoul had feasted here.

The sheriff arrived with lights and sirens.

"Want me to handle him?" Brax asked, and I bristled immediately.

"No. You can go. This,"—I waved my arm toward Mrs. B—"confirms what we already guessed. Go back over our research, specifically at the recent missing persons, and see if we can tie him in with the time he discarded this body and took the next."

"Agent Shelton." The sheriff touched the brim of his hat in greeting. "Where's the body?"

"Here. From the height and clothing, I'm going to assume it's Mrs. B. I hear she's been missing a few days."

The sheriff peered into the grave, wiped his hand over his nose, then stepped back. He spoke into the radio clipped to his shoulder, requesting the coroner's van for pick-up.

"How did you find it?" he asked, hands-on-hips while he surveyed the area.

"Searching for something else, and one of my agents came across her," I replied.

"One of your agents? Who? I may need to talk to them." He pulled out a notebook, ready to take names.

"You may remember her? Rae Shelton?" I knew the history between Rae and the sheriff. It wasn't good. He sputtered, and his cheeks turned red.

"What? Rae's back?"

"She is. She's an SIA Agent now, so it's time you two learned to get along. A lot has happened that you don't know about—and you don't need to know, so don't even ask. And before we go on, yes, this is a supernatural kill. I'll tell you what killed her if you really want to know, but otherwise, I'd say you could file this under animal attack if it weren't for the fact her body has been dumped in a shallow grave."

"Wild dogs. A dog owner thought it was their dog and panicked, tried to hide the body," he responded, deadpan.

"I'll leave you to it." With a nod, I walked back to my truck, lost in thought. Mrs. B had been our last link to Stillwater Pharmaceuticals. They'd cleared out the drugs Nate had found; everything looked above board—on the surface.

"Wait." I spun and headed back toward the sheriff, who was looking at Mrs. B with sad eyes. "Have you seen this woman?" I swiped through my phone and pulled up a picture of Ridgeway and held it out. He squinted at the screen, then shook his head.

"Nope. But send it to me. I can pass it around the station and tell the guys to keep an eye out."

"Thank you." This time, my smile was sincere.

"I take it she's the one you're after? The one who is responsible for this?"

"Indirectly, yes."

"And she's paranormal?"

"A shifter. Don't approach her if you see her. Consider her to be armed and dangerous. Just call me. If any of your crew sees her, call me." With a heavy heart, I headed back to my truck. Paige was going to be devastated at the news of Mrs. B's death. Although she knew, technically, that Mrs. B. was already dead when the ghoul took possession of her body, now it was real. Now it was tangible.

The buzzing of my cell phone was a welcome relief from the sounds coming through the wall from Rae's bedroom. Through sleep-deprived eyes, I squinted at the screen. Sheriff Brady calling in the middle of the night couldn't be good.

"Shelton," I answered.

"Think I've got something for you," Sheriff Brady said.

"Oh?" Sitting up, I clicked on the bedside lamp and glanced at the clock. Just gone two a.m. "A sighting on Ridgeway?" I asked hopefully.

"Nope. A missing person. A kidnapping, you might call it."

"And this happened tonight?"

"Affirmative. I've got a very hysterical young woman here who says they were driving home when they came across a body lying on the road. Her boyfriend was driving; he stopped and got out to check. She dropped her phone, bent to pick it up, and when she looked up, they were both gone. No body. No boyfriend." He paused, then added, "No signs of a struggle, no blood, nothing to go on except her story. Sound like something you'd be interested in?"

"Yes. I'm on my way. Are you still on the scene?"

"Yeah. I'll wait for you." He gave me the address, a dark, deserted road about ten minutes out of town. The perfect place for a vampire to snatch a victim. Pulling on jeans and a tank, I swept up my keys and headed out.

The night was dark, clouds covered any light the moon may have provided, and as I pulled up behind the sheriff's vehicle, I glanced around. The perfect spot for an ambush. Dark and deserted, with thick vegetation on either side of the road.

I made my way to where a young woman was sitting in the passenger seat of the sheriff's car, the door open, her sniffling sobs carrying on the night air.

"Hi." I approached with a smile; she was spooked enough as it was. "My name is Katie. I'm a special agent. Can you tell me what happened here tonight?"

She looked up at me, her pale face smeared with mascara, her nose red, bundles of tissues clenched in her fists.

"Braden and I were coming home from a party at Jesse's place. It was getting late, and I've got work in the morning. Anyway, Braden said if we take the Old Mill Road, it will save us some time, and I was arguing because it shaves, what, two seconds off the trip? But I think it's a boy thing, that they like the bends and curves up here and the extra challenge because it's so damn dark you can't see if an animal is on the road until you're practically on top of it."

"Take a breath." I patted her shoulder. "What's your name?"

"Amy." She hiccupped, dragging in a deep breath, her shoulders shaking.

"You're doing great, Amy. So Braden was driving. Were you fighting?"

"Not really." She shrugged, "Not angry arguing, just discussing whether Old Mill Road was the shortest route after all? I'd have taken Hadly

Crossing; we were debating it, I guess you could say."

"And then what happened?"

"We came around the corner." She pointed to the curve just behind us. "And there was something on the road. Something lying down. I thought it was a dead animal, and I screamed at Braden to watch out. He hit the brakes, and we stopped, and he said he'd better clear it off the road in case someone else came around the corner and hit it."

"So, he got out to move it. Could you see what it was?"

She looked at me with shiny, terrified eyes. "It was a man. Once we'd stopped and our headlights were right on it, I could see it was a man. He had dark pants, cowboy boots, and a long coat—I mean, who wears a coat in Maxxan? It's hot twenty-four-seven! And a hat, a Stetson that was laid over his face, and he was just lying there."

"And Braden got out to check, see if he was alive?"

She nodded, sniffing. "Yes. He yelled for me to call 911, and my hands were shaking so badly that I dropped my phone. I bent to pick it up, and when I looked back up, they'd gone. It was only a second. Where could they have gone?"

"Then what did you do?" She had that wild look about her, the one that said she was scared out of her mind and couldn't make sense of what she'd seen.

"I got out of the car and screamed for Braden." She turned and looked out the windshield as if she could see him now. "But he didn't answer. It was really quiet, no night noises, just the sound of the engine running. I came around to the front of the car because the man had been lying on the road right in front of us, but he was gone too. There was nothing there. No blood. Nothing. I can't remember much else after that. I think I panicked. I was screaming for Braden and running back and forth a bit, looking for him at the side of the road, but I couldn't find him."

"You've done great, Amy, thank you. I'm going to get the sheriff to take care of you now, okay?" Knowing she was paying scant attention to me, I patted her arm, her mind struggling to comprehend what had happened here tonight.

Leaving her in the sheriff's car, I walked up to where he waited in front of Braden's vehicle. The engine had been turned off; the headlights left on to light the way.

"What do you think?" the sheriff asked, leaning

back against the hood and looking out into the darkness.

"Vampire, for sure." I kept my voice low so that Amy wouldn't overhear.

"Figured it was something paranormal. No way an animal could have dragged him off that fast, not without a scream, a fight, or a blood trail."

"You know that's what you're going to have to tell her, though. That an animal took him."

"Yeah, I know." He sighed a heavy, weary sigh. "Right then, I'll get the car towed and take Amy to the hospital, get her checked out. The rest I'll leave for you. Maybe it won't be such a bad thing having the SIA in town after all."

"Thanks."

I waited until the sheriff had left with Amy. The tow truck would be here soon; they'd be taking Braden's car to the compound. I didn't need it; it would contain no evidence of what had happened here tonight, but what did interest me was the description Amy had given of the vampire who had taken her boyfriend. Cowboy boots. Long coat. Stetson hat. *Could it be the Gunslinger?* But what would the Gunslinger be doing back in Maxxan? The Red Witch had broken the spell that had allowed vampires to walk in the daylight; the drug crops were gone—what could he be doing here?

I laughed softly to myself. I was guessing; it probably wasn't the Gunslinger at all. All I had to go on was the confused recollection of a hysterical woman whose boyfriend had been snatched by a vampire. And experience told me people in shock didn't recall details as clearly as they think they did. The Stetson could turn out to be a baseball cap. The boots could have been sneakers. The coat, though? She seemed pretty sure of what she'd seen.

Pulling out my phone, I hit speed dial.

"Is this a booty call?" Brax drawled, his voice thick with sleep, "Because if it is, I'm all for it. The answer is yes."

My whole body flushed at his words, and I had to bite my tongue from saying yes. Instead, I said, "We've got a case. A vampire attack."

"Where?" He was all business; I could hear rustling in the background and pictured him throwing back the bedcovers, sitting up, naked. Urgh, the mental images were killing me. Memories flooded me, his body against mine, skin to skin, his hands on me, caressing, his mouth following the path his hands had taken. I groaned.

"Katie?"

Brax's voice down the line snapped me out of my sensual haze, and I quickly gave directions to Old Mill Road, glad he couldn't see the flush in my cheeks. He'd know—and give me hell.

I was scouring the foliage by the side of the road when he arrived, searching for...anything really. A bent twig to indicate someone had crouched here, a torn piece of clothing that had caught on a branch, but I came up with nothing.

"You're positive this is a vampire?" Brax asked after I'd filled him in.

"Well, it's a classic MO. Hear a car coming. Pretend to be dead on the road. Wait while the intended victim gets out and approaches, and then bam. Come on; it's a classic vamp move. Even *The Vampire Diaries* does it."

"You watch *The Vampire Diaries*?" His laugh held a hint of surprise.

"Don't tell me you haven't seen an episode or two. I won't believe you, even if you deny it," I mocked.

"What's your favorite TV show?"

"Why?"

He shrugged. "No reason, just wondered."

I watched him with narrowed eyes, unsure of his

motives. *Who cares what my favorite TV show is?* Then it hit me. He was getting to know me.

"No. This stops. This stops now!"

"You can't stop it, Katie." He knew exactly what I was talking about, and it scared the hell out of me that he was that in tune with me. He stalked toward me, eyes dark and intent, and I swallowed. There was something about this man that made me weak at the knees, that made me want to throw caution to the wind, that made me want to strip him naked and make him mine. But such thoughts were crazy dangerous, and I'd made up my mind that there would be no more sex with this man, despite the mind-blowing effect he had on me. Absolutely not.

Standing my ground, I concentrated on breathing as he approached. A tingling of anticipation thundered through my veins; arousal leaped inside me so fast I felt the world spin. Yet I didn't move, couldn't move.

Brax raised a hand to my face. The heat that emanated from him caressed me like hot silk. He was a fire demon, like me, and I welcomed his heat, reveled in it, wanted to rub my cheek against his palm and purr like a kitten.

"I have a plan." His hot breath against my lips made

my pulse flare. "A plan to get to know you, body and soul, inside and out—and nothing you can do or say is going to discourage me from that course of action." He paused, his palm slowly sliding around to my nape, the frisson of awareness electrifying. I had the devil on one shoulder and an angel on the other. I wanted him. Physically, there was no doubting I wanted him. I craved him; the way his hair tussled beneath my fingers, the reverent way he touched me, the sensations he could coax from me. All of that was indisputable proof of how much I wanted him. But it was sex. Chemistry. And that was all I could offer him, ever.

And Brax Lane wanted more. Oh, he hadn't said it. *Yet*. But I knew. It was in the way he touched me, the way his eyes devoured me. And that scared me more than any monster on earth.

"Stop thinking." His lips hovered above mine. "Just feel." And then he lowered his mouth to mine, fusing us together. The heat was blistering and surreal, and I felt it all the way to my toes. He broke off the kiss and nipped at my ear. "Just feel."

Wrapping my arms around his neck, I gave in. I surrendered to the heat, and my surrender was intoxicating. Pressing my mouth to his, I was lost. He fought a smile for a moment, returned my kiss enthusiastically, then backed me against his car.

One hand wrapped around my nape, his long fingers pulling at the short strands of my hair, while the other hand slipped beneath my shirt, then slid around my waist and up my spine, his fingers tracing the hollow line of my vertebrae.

I pulled him closer. He let a husky growl escape him; the deep sound reverberated through my bones. The time for words was over. I wanted this man, all of him.

Tearing my mouth from his intoxicating kiss, I tugged at his shirt. He obligingly pulled it over his head, tossing it over his shoulder. My hands ran over him, exploring the hills and valleys of his muscles as they contracted and released under my touch. I felt the smoothness of his skin, the hardness of his muscles, the tautness of his abdomen.

Brax dipped his head, kissing me again with an intensity that took my breath away. Any last vestiges of resistance were gone, evaporating in the searing heat of that kiss.

Then, our hands were everywhere. Tearing at clothing in our haste, sensations overpowering, the world outside of us disappearing as we lost ourselves in each other. I held him to me, immersed in his essence, in his taste, texture, and scent. The night air caressed my skin, the faint sounds of nightlife reached my ears, and for a brief moment, I was at peace.

"I don't know what all this means," Brax murmured, lifting his head to rest his forehead against mine, "but I think I may be falling for you, Katie." It was a bucket of cold water over my overheated flesh. I froze, then pushed him away, the movement catching him by surprise and making him stagger. I had to get away from him and the damn spell he seemed to cast over me every time he was near. *He was dangerous.*

Angrily, I hurried back to my truck, hobbling as I clutched my boots against my chest, trying to dress as I walked. How had he managed to get me naked so fast?

"Katie! Wait, wait, Katie." I kept going, cursing when a stone dug into the sole of my foot. I hopped to dislodge it, then picked up the pace as I heard him dressing behind me.

"Stop!"

I didn't.

"Stop, Katie." He slammed his fist on the hood of his car, and I jumped. "Please." I was at my truck, opening the door, climbing inside.

"I'm sorry, okay? What do you think? That I

meant to fall for someone who's made it clear they're not interested!"

I looked at him through my windshield, my vision unexpectedly blurry. In silence, I turned the key, shoved the truck into gear, and sped away, leaving him half-naked on Old Mill Road.

"He did what?" Rae's voice dripped with mock outrage. "How dare he tell you he's falling for you."

"Shut up." We were at Stanley's. I'd spent the whole day avoiding Brax, and it hadn't been easy because he'd spent the entire day trying to get me alone. When Jordan had suggested taking Bear out to Old Mill Road to see if he could pick up a scent, I'd told him to take Brax with him. As soon as they'd gone, I'd dragged Rae to Stanley's.

"I know what you're thinking. That Brax Lane is stupid hot," I said into my beer.

Rae snorted. "Not as hot as Jordan, but okay."

"And the sex? Oh god, Rae, the sex is..."

"Amazing? Out of this world? Incredible?" Rae supplied with a grin.

"All of those things," I admitted.

"Because you two have chemistry. You know you don't get that sort of chemistry with just any man, right?"

My shoulders slumped. "I know." And I did. Brax wasn't the first man I'd slept with after Ethan had died. But he was the only man who had made me come alive, who'd made me feel. With the others, I'd been going through the motions, and it had felt... nice. Which made it easy to walk away. That had been my motto, and it had worked really well until now.

"But seriously, Katie." Rae touched my arm, and I glanced at her, her face sincere and a little sad. "Why is that a bad thing?"

"Because I couldn't bear for it to happen again." My eyes welled at the remembered pain of losing my family. My heart had been ripped from my chest that day, and I'd never survive it happening again. I couldn't risk it. Wouldn't risk it.

"Oh, Katie." Rae hugged me; I didn't need to explain any further. She got it. "I'm so sorry, hon."

"Wanna do shots?" I sniffed with a watery smile.

"Sure."

And that's why, when Brax and Jordan found us a couple of hours later, I was dancing on the bar. Duke kept feeding the jukebox quarters, and as long as the tunes were playing, I was dancing.

"How long has she been like this?" I heard Brax ask Rae.

"She's fine. Leave her alone," Rae replied, reaching up to kiss Jordan full on the mouth.

"Did I break her?" Brax muttered. "I didn't mean to break her."

"She's not broken. She's a Shelton, a tough one." Rae poked him in the shoulder. "You need to slow your roll, dude. You're coming on strong, and that is what's freaking her out."

"But I—"

"Nuh-uh!" Rae cut him off. "Slow down. Give her time. You know about her fiancé and kid, right?"

"What?" By the stunned expression on his face, I assumed he hadn't heard. I stopped dancing and jumped down from the bar.

"Rae," I warned.

"Oops. Busted." Rae grinned. "Come on, Jordan, let's dance." Grabbing Jordan by the hand, she pulled him over to the jukebox and wrapped her arms around his neck, her body flush with his, and the pair of them began swaying to the rhythm.

"You've got a fiancé?" Brax asked, his voice at least three octaves higher than usual. "And a kid?"

"Had."

"What, you're separated, and he has custody? Because that's okay, Katie. I can deal with that. I love kids. Can't wait to have my own one day."

"They're dead."

He looked at me in stunned silence. I ordered another shot and slammed it down, the alcohol burning and numbing at the same time. But all the alcohol in the world couldn't take away the pain of losing Ethan and Abigail. In Redmeadows, I'd done an excellent job of almost forgetting, but here in Maxxan, they were everywhere. Memories. They consumed me, just as my lust for Brax consumed me. It was exhausting.

"I'm so sorry." He rested a hand on my shoulder, and I shrugged him away.

"Don't."

"What happened? How did they die?"

"I killed them." I walked away, and he let me go. For it was true, I had killed them. I'd been behind the wheel of the car that day. I was the driver. I was responsible. They were dead because of me.

"Katie. Wait."

"Leave her be, Brax." This time it was Jordan,

and I suspected he was holding Brax back from following me. Of course, Jordan would know. Rae would have filled him in on my tragic past.

Duke caught up with me outside. "You're not driving, young lady." He slammed his hand against my truck door to stop me from opening it.

"Fuck off, Duke," I snapped.

"You're wasted. And angry. Not a good combo to get behind the wheel." His words were a slap in the face, and I gasped, my hand going to my chest.

"Ah man, I didn't mean that the way it sounded," Duke swore, then caught my hand in his. "Come on, Katie, I'll drive you home." I let him lead me to his truck, climbing inside and waiting while he buckled me in since, suddenly, I was incapable.

"I don't want to go home," I said when he slid behind the wheel.

"Where do you want to go?" The engine rumbled to life, and he flicked the headlights on.

"Paige's apartment. I can't sleep at home. Rae and Jordan are going at it like rabbits every bloody night. You'd think they'd have had enough by now," I grumbled.

Duke laughed but refrained from comment other than to say, "Paige's place it is."

Paige's apartment was above the bakery, and

when I'd talked to her earlier in the day and complained about my sleeping issues—mainly that I wasn't getting any due to Rae's sexathons every damn night—Paige had offered up her apartment since she wasn't using it while she was in Redmeadows.

Duke walked me up the stairs, retrieved the spare key from where Paige had hidden it, unlocked the door, and ushered me inside. The apartment was small but cozy small, not claustrophobic small. It was cute, and I liked it.

"You okay from here?" Duke asked from the doorway.

"Sure. You go. Thanks for being a good friend." I waved him away, and he left, closing the door with a soft click. I flicked the deadbolt and made my way to the bedroom. Flopping down onto the bed, I slept.

Sleep was not the usual slumber I was used to. Since returning to Maxxan, my dreams have been haunted by the past, and I woke up crying, shaking, and distressed. Tonight was no different. I'd been blaming my sleep deprivation on Rae and Jordan's antics, but that wasn't entirely true.

Sitting up, I pushed my hair out of my eyes. I was sober now. I hadn't been as drunk as everyone assumed, but I had been exhausted, and the few hours of sleep I'd managed to snatch had revived me. A little, anyway.

After a hot shower, I borrowed a pair of Paige's shorts and a top and hit the kitchen. I loved to bake. It was my thing, and I hadn't done it in a long time. Raiding Paige's fridge, I began a shopping list. Paige was not one to cook. She was a takeout kind of girl, so my shopping list was long. But she had a handful of essentials, and I made do, and for the first time in a long time, I felt normal. Almost happy. Baking in the kitchen in the early hours while the rest of the world slept.

"These cookies are great!" Duke stuffed another one in his mouth, not taking his eyes off the screen where we were battling it out in *Destiny 2*. I had a strike team assembled, and we were about to kick Duke's ass.

"Distraction tactics won't work, Ellis." I grinned. "You're toast!"

I directed my on-screen character to duck behind the burned-out remnants of a truck while I reloaded. Damn, almost out of ammo. I scoured for an ammo pack, spotted one nearby, dodged the mother of all robots to retrieve it, and then blew Duke's character to kingdom come.

"Oh man," Duke complained, tossing his

controller onto the couch between us, "you're too friggin' good at this."

"Told you I had skills."

"Move over, Duke, my turn." Jordan snatched up the controller and squeezed in between Duke and me. It had been a slow day at work. Jordan and Brax had taken Bear out to Old Mill Road, and all he'd found was my discarded underwear. My face had burned with embarrassment when Brax had held them up in front of me like a trophy. I'd gone to snatch them from him, but he'd tucked them into his back pocket before winking at me and taking a seat at his workstation.

Rae and Jordan had laughed. Long and loud. And finally, I let myself relax, just a little. It was no secret Brax, and I were sleeping together. I'd been avoiding labeling it, had been telling myself he was just a one-night stand, but one night had multiplied alarmingly until I couldn't ignore it anymore. We may not be a couple, not in the sense that Brax wanted us to be, but we were sleeping together. And despite him saying he was falling for me, I couldn't stay away. He was like a damn magnet.

At the end of our shift, I'd diverted the phones to my cell and invited everyone to Paige's apartment to play video games. Soaking my liver in alcohol every night wasn't the most brilliant move if I wanted to stay sharp and catch Ridgeway—and the Gunslinger if he was in town. And sometimes, when I'm fully immersed in a game, my mind does its thing. It goes off and solves the puzzles I've been pondering. Tonight, I was hoping for a win, game-wise and case-wise.

"Jesus, Katie!" Jordan complained. "Give a guy a chance, would you?" He'd only just joined the game, and I'd killed him.

"You snooze, you lose," I smirked.

"Here." Rae snatched the controller from him and sat on his lap. "Bitch, bring it," she said to me. Duke groaned at being pinned in the corner of the sofa and wriggled out, so Jordan scooted over and deposited Rae next to me. I hit play on the game and tuned them all out, the shouts and yahoos, the tips to both Rae and me on what our next move should be. Ignoring them all, I concentrated on my character on the screen and went with my gut.

"Crazy, awesome, bitch!" Rae laughed at the demise of her character. "God, I need a drink. That was intense." Slinging her arm around my shoulder, she swiveled her head, her eyes zeroing in on Brax, who'd dragged a kitchen chair over and had straddled it, his arms resting along the back.

"Brax, grab us a couple of beers, will ya?"

The apartment was that small he merely leaned back, flipped open the fridge door, and grabbed two beers, passing them over to us.

"Thanks." I nodded to him, not sure how to act around him now that he'd told me he had feelings. Popping the top off the beer, I took a long swig.

"Here, Brax, your turn to take on the champion." Rae handed him the controller. He took it and looked at me, his eyes intent, quizzical.

"Think you can take me?" he drawled. Oh, the challenge was undeniable. As was the double entendre.

"You think you've got what it takes?" I replied, surprising myself. Was I *flirting?*

"You betcha sweet ass, I do." Sitting his beer on the floor, he grasped the controller in both hands, turned his eyes to the screen, and waited for me to reload the game. I put my beer on the coffee table, cracked my neck, rolled my shoulders, and hit play.

My game with Rae had been intense—she was good, and I'd had to concentrate on taking her down, but I knew that eventually, I'd win. But Brax? He kicked my ass. Every move I made, he had a countermove. He knew what I was going to do before I did it, anticipating and cutting me off. Until there it was, my character flashing red on the screen.

Jordan and Duke were crazy loud with their hooting and celebrating my demise, and I laughed. Who knew having my ass handed to me would actually feel good?

Tossing the controller onto the coffee table, I stood up and stretched. "Thanks for a great game." I smiled at Brax, then looked at the group gathered in Paige's tiny apartment. "So, who wants pizza?"

"Only if you're making it," Rae replied, quick as a flash. She turned to Jordan. "In case you didn't know, my cousin here is a genius in the kitchen. Gee-nee-us! Those cookies? Pft, they're just the start. You guys,"—she looked between Jordan, Brax, and Duke—"you seriously want her pizza, I tell you."

"She's right, man," Duke added. "This girl can make toast taste like angel food cake."

"With a build-up like that, you'd better not disappoint, Shelton," Jordan teased.

Leaving them to continue with the game, I took my beer into the kitchen and began making dinner. I'd swung by the grocery store after work, and now the kitchen cupboards and refrigerator were bulging with food.

"Can I help?" Brax spoke into my ear, and I jumped. I hadn't heard him approach over the noise of the others. Looking at him over my shoulder, I nodded. "Sure. Cut this up, will you?" And handed him a stick of salami. "Thin slices. Thin," I instructed.

Side by side, we worked in silence. And it was comfortable. It was nice. And I was doing my best not to freak out—it wasn't easy.

"Nothing to do now but wait," I said, sliding two pizzas into the oven and dusting my hands on the back of my jeans.

"Katie." He was doing it again, saying my name in that mesmerizing way of his, making me want him. He leaned in close. "Duke's been trying to get your attention for the last...ohhhh, ten minutes or so."

My eyes shot over his shoulder to where Duke was eyeballing me from across the room, an empty bottle of beer dangling from his fingers.

"Finally!" he drawled, rolling his eyes. "You're a lousy hostess, Shelton. Now bring me a beer, woman." I felt my cheeks heat, not at Duke's teasing, but the fact that I had been so engrossed and focused on Brax that the rest of the world had ceased to exist. My eyes shot to Brax, and his stupid, sexy smirk got the best of me. I weakened. I kissed him on the cheek, then pushed him to one side to get Duke his drink. *What on earth are you doing, Katie Shelton?*

The pizzas were a success, as I knew they would be, and everyone left with full stomachs and a smile on their face. After walking Duke, Jordan, and Rae out, I turned to Brax, who was standing with his keys in hand.

"You're going?" I hadn't expected him to leave; the fact that he intended to took me by surprise.

"I've figured something out about you, Katie Shelton." He tucked a strand of hair behind my ear and smiled. "I'm pretty sure you just want me for my body. And who can blame you? I'm a magnificent specimen; you can't deny it. And you already know that I know how to please a lady in the bedroom. Oh yeah. I know where to touch, how to touch, and most importantly, when to touch." His words vibrated through me and made my knees tremble because every word he spoke was true.

He opened his mouth to continue, but I cut him off. Pulling his head down, I planted my lips on his and kissed him. He growled, and I squirmed in delight. He was quickly becoming my obsession, and if this was madness, maybe I didn't want to be cured. Slowly, he ended the kiss, his lips lingering for a second. "But," he continued, his voice low and deep and smoldering, "I'm cutting you off."

"What?" I was stunned. Was he...breaking up with me? Even though we weren't a couple?

"No more meaningless sex." He nodded, cupping my face. I don't know why, but I wanted to cry. Where was this emotion coming from? It was confusing and confronting, and I didn't like it.

"You can have all the sex you want...as soon as you agree to date me."

"Date you?" I spluttered, ignoring the wave of relief that crashed over me. He wasn't breaking up with me. But he was issuing ultimatums. And I didn't like that either.

"You and me. Dinner. Alone—without your team of chaperones. Don't think I haven't noticed you've either got Duke, Rae, or Jordan with you, a buffer between us. I want you. I want you so badly I ache, and I know you want me too."

"But you want more," I whispered, the fear in my voice real. I couldn't offer him more.

"I want all of you," he agreed, rubbing his thumb along my jaw, making me turn my head into his hand and rub, begging for more contact. And then he dropped his hand, stepped back, and smiled, a bright, dazzling smile. My head was spinning.

"Let me know when you're ready for that date, and I promise, at the end of it, I will fu—"

"No!" I knew what he was about to say. He'd fuck me anyway I wanted. He was using sex as a currency. He was using sex to get what he wanted.

"Not going to happen. Night, Brax, thanks for coming." I held the door open for him, and he walked through. The door slammed behind him.

I was working on the case board, trying to piece together the autopsy results with the potential cause of death. Vampires took up one side of the board, ghouls on the other, with a smattering of possible wolf shifter attacks in the center, although the wolf kills were always hard to differentiate from an actual wild animal attack.

My phone rang at the same time that Brax's did, and we looked at each other in surprise.

"Shelton," I answered as Brax simultaneously picked up his call.

"We've got something for you." It was the tech from Redmeadows HQ, the one who was doing the in-depth forensic analysis of Stillwater Pharmaceuticals' digital records.

"Excellent, we could use a lead. Whatcha got?"

"I'm not sure you're going to like it." The tech hedged, and I glanced at Brax, who was watching me with a frown while he listened to whoever was on the other end of his call.

"Tell me anyway," I prompted, watching as Brax pushed out of his chair, voice low as he continued his call outside.

The tech blew out a breath, then launched into his report. "There was a visitor to the facility who signed in at least six times. The person at the facility they signed in to visit doesn't exist."

"They gave a fake name of who they had come to see?" Why wouldn't he want to tell me that?

"Yes. A different fake name each time."

"Who was it?"

"The fake names?"

"No. The visitor. Who was visiting the facility?"

There was a pause, then, "Ethan McMahon."

I pulled the phone from my ear and looked at it. Had I heard right?

"Did you say, McMahon? Ethan McMahon?"

"Affirmative."

"As in, my fiancé Ethan McMahon? My dead fiancé." I was glad Brax had decided to take his call outside. I didn't want him to overhear this.

"Yes, ma'am."

I digested what he'd said, leaned back in my chair, and stared up at the ceiling, trying to form some sort of thought process, but I came up blank. Eventually, the tech cleared his throat. "You still there?" he asked.

"Er, yeah. Sorry. Okay. Well, give me the rest—and can you email me your report as well, please? I'm a little stunned here; I don't want to miss anything."

"Not a problem. So, McMahon's visits ceased three years ago. Before that, it was once or twice a year, over six years. Each time he filled in the visitor's log, he put a different fake name of who he was there to see." They'd stopped three years ago because he'd died.

"Yet they let him in. They must have known who he was visiting and what he was doing there. The fake names were for this type of thing—the authorities searching."

"Yes."

"Can you cross-reference all the employees' calendars and match any appointments with the times of his visits? Let's see if we can work out who he was seeing—and what he was doing there."

"Already on it. Hope to get something to you today."

"Thank you. And thank you for calling with the update. I appreciate it."

"You're welcome. I'm sorry McMahon is involved."

"Me too." I hung up, then stared at my monitor. The report from the tech arrived, flashing at me from my inbox. I didn't open it.

Brax came back in, sat at his desk, typed something on his laptop, and then blew out a breath. "Katie, there's no easy way to say this," he began, his voice pained, "but it looks like your fiancé may have been involved in this."

"I know," I said, not meeting his eyes. "Our tech just called. I guess the Secret Service got the report at the same time, huh?"

"I'm sorry."

I shrugged. "It's not your fault. Anyway, we don't know what it means; he could have been there on legitimate business." Ethan had been a paramedic; it was entirely possible he was there in an official capacity.

"It's the fake names that give us concern."

"I know. Look, our tech is cross-referencing records as we speak. There's no point in your people doing the same work. Unless you don't trust me? Since I was his fiancé?"

"What? No! Of course, I trust you." He seemed genuinely surprised I'd think otherwise, but I wouldn't have blamed him if he'd had doubts. This case had taken a very personal turn, one I hadn't anticipated. If our roles were reversed and a suspect turned out to be personally connected to him, I'd question his presence in Maxxan and objectivity in working the case.

Speaking of, I picked up my phone and dialed.

"Do you want me off the case?" I asked Nate as soon as he answered.

"No. I trust you can stay objective. Do you want off the case?"

"No."

"Good." And he hung up. I laughed, the sound bordering on hysterical. Bad news carries fast. The next thing, both Rae and Jordan came storming in, demanding to know if I was okay.

"Okay, listen up, all of you! Rae and Jordan, sit." I pointed to their workstations, then stood by the case board. "First of all, to allay all your fears, I'm fine. I'm shocked but fine. And I don't believe Ethan was involved, not knowingly, and it's up to us to prove that. Tech is working on finding out who it was he was visiting at Stillwater. After all, if he had something to hide, he would have used a fake name to protect himself. But he didn't, so I'm taking that to mean that whatever he was doing there, as far as he was concerned, it was legit.

"Rae, I want you to go to the coroner's office and see if they have blood or tissue samples on these victims." I pointed to the board. "If they do, get them to the lab and have them run tests on the compound Nate retrieved from Stillwater. See if we have any matches. Brax and Jordan, I want you to interview any employees who have been with Stillwater for longer than five years—specifically in the six-to-seven-years-ago range. Take a photo of Ethan with you and see if they recall seeing him at the facility. I'm not waiting on tech for this. We've been waiting days for a break, and this is it. Let's run with it."

"Yes, boss." There was a flurry of activity and then blessed silence. They were gone, and I was finally alone. Holding my breath, I clicked open the report the tech had sent and steeled myself, but nothing could have prepared me for seeing Ethan's smiling face appear on my screen.

My heart ached. A physical ache that had me rubbing at the center of my chest. I looked into the blue eyes of the man I had loved and lost, my heart yearning to be with him again, see him smile, feel his arms around me, longing for just one more moment. Something wet dripped onto the back of my hand, and I glanced up at the ceiling. *Don't tell me we have a bloody water leak.* But the ceiling was dry, and then I realized it was me. I was crying. Wiping the tears away with the back of my hand, I pulled up Lani's number and dialed.

"Hey, Katie," she answered straight away, her bright and bubbly voice not so bright or bubbly. The sheriff had delivered the news of her mother's death after we'd found her body a couple of days ago. I'd been meaning to call her but had been avoiding it—now it was time to man up and get on with things.

"I'm so sorry about your mom, Lani," I said. "She was a great woman who will be sadly missed."

"Thank you." She sniffed. I knew what it was like. People telling you they were sorry someone you loved had died. Sorry didn't cut it. Sorry didn't help with the pain.

"When's the funeral?" I asked.

"Day after tomorrow. You coming?"

"Of course. I'm sorry Paige can't come. She's been held up in Redmeadows. She'd be here if she could." The truth was Nate had decided not to tell her about the discovery of Mrs. B's body. He knew she'd want to come home and be with her friend, but he wasn't prepared to put her in harm's way. It wasn't that I necessarily agreed with him—I didn't like keeping secrets from those I loved, but it was safer in this case. Ridgeway would snatch Paige the first chance she got; I was sure of it. As far as we could tell, Paige was the first candidate who had survived the toxic drug they'd pumped into her. They'd want her back to continue with the experiment.

"I can't believe she's gone," Lani whispered.

"Me either." I paused. "Look, I know this is a terrible time...but I need your help."

"Oh?"

"The sheriff told you that he thought your mom was murdered, didn't he?"

"Yes. The shallow grave. That they must have been interrupted before they could bury her, so they took off, leaving her exposed. And the animals got to her."

"If it's okay with you, I'd like to go through your mom's stuff. See if I can find any clue as to what happened to her."

"Are you working for the sheriff now?" Lani

quizzed, remembering that I used to be a deputy here in Maxxan.

"Not directly. I work with a special agency in Redmeadows. I'm here on a case, but we're working closely with the sheriff's office."

"And your case…is that connected to my mom?"

"There's a possibility it could be. I don't know for sure, which is why I'd like to go through your mom's stuff to see if I can find a connection."

"Then yes. Of course. I want the bastards who did this caught."

"Me too," I assured her. Lani was human, and there was only so much I could tell her. While I hated to deceive my sister's best friend, the truth was her mom's link to Stillwater Pharmaceuticals was vital. A ghoul had chosen her—she'd been dead for weeks, possibly months, with the ghoul wearing her skin like a suit. Now that the ghoul had moved on, I needed to know why—and who they were wearing now. "Is it okay if I come now? The quicker we move on this, the better."

"Yes, of course. I'm here. I've got the week off work."

Which reminded me that Lani was mourning, that the loss of her mom was real and raw. "Can I bring you anything? Pick up anything on my way over? Have you eaten?"

She laughed. "My refrigerator is overflowing with casseroles. I'm good for a month, I reckon."

"Beer?"

"Beer would be perfect."

"See you in a few." Sliding my swipe card into my back pocket, I picked up my keys and headed out, making sure I swung by the store to pick up a six-pack of beer on the way.

TWELVE

Jordan had already searched Mrs. B's house, which saved me considerable time and effort. What I was looking for wouldn't be left lying around. It would be small, inconsequential, something easily overlooked, something the ghoul hadn't thought to be of any consequence. Of course, I had no idea what that might be; I was just hoping against hope that I'd find something, anything, that would move the investigation forward.

"Is there anything missing?" I asked Lani as we stood in her mother's living room. It had that empty feeling of neglect; you could smell it on the stale air, the layer of dust coating the furniture. Mrs. B hadn't been in residence for some time—longer than the week she'd been dead.

"Missing? Well, no, not that I know of. Why, do you think someone broke in?"

"No, no, nothing like that. Is there anything that is usually here that isn't anymore? Cell phone? Laptop? Car keys? Diary? That sort of thing."

"Oh…I'll have to look; I hadn't really checked. Mom has a home office set up in the spare room; I could take a look, see if anything is missing if you like?"

"That'd be great. I'm going to take a walk around outside and see if there's anything out of the ordinary, okay?"

"Sure." I waited until Lani disappeared down the hallway before opening the back door and stepping out onto the deck. The heat was relentless, and today was no different. The back of Mrs. B's house copped the majority of the sun, and with high side fences, it felt like the heat was trapped against the house, stifling in its intensity. Sliding on my sunglasses, I stepped down onto the dead lawn, the shriveled blades of grass crunching loudly beneath my boots.

Moving among the remnants of the garden, I noted that the garden was a clue in itself, for obviously, this had once been a thriving garden. Yet, now the shrubs and flowers were dead. It would have taken a few weeks of neglect for them to get to this state, so Mrs. B had been consumed by the ghoul some time ago, as we'd suspected. Paige had meant well when she'd pulled up Mrs. B's file when she and Nate had broken into the facility, but it had indicated they'd been discovered, and the record subsequently scrubbed. But Lani had said her mom had been promoted after she'd gone to Redmeadows for some conference. That's when we think the swap happened. That's when Mrs. B really died.

There were no more clues to be had, so I stood and looked at the house before my eyes settled on the garage. It was a separate building, not attached to the main house, designed for a single car with a pull-up door and no side entrance. With a heave, I pulled the door up and pushed it on the sliders that squeaked in protest. It had either not been used in a while or was severely in need of maintenance, and from what I could see from Mrs. B's house, she wasn't one to let things fall into disrepair. So why then, was the garage door so goddamn hard to open?

Inside was her car. It only just fit, squeezed in along with a lawnmower and gardening tools, plus boxes stacked neatly at one end. I couldn't get to the boxes with the car in the way. I tried to squeeze through, but it was no good, and I had to back out, my clothes now covered in dust from the car. Patting myself down, I coughed at the cloud of red that enveloped me.

"Oh, there it is," Lani said. I swiveled to see her standing in the driveway.

"What?"

"Mom's car. I thought maybe it was at work or something. I didn't look here."

"So, it's not usual for it to be in the garage?"

She shook her head. "She usually parked it under the carport. The garage is for storage and garden crap."

"Do you know what's in the boxes?" I pointed, and Lani grinned.

"Yeah, my shit from when I was a kid. Mom didn't like to throw any of it out, so she would box it up every couple of years and put it in here. My whole childhood is in those boxes."

"Right." Doubtful the boxes would hold anything of use. I made a mental note to get Jordan or Rae to go through them. And that's when I noticed it. Why I hadn't before was beyond me, but I was wiping my dusty palms on my pants and frowning at the red dust marks when it became blatantly obvious. Maxxan didn't have red dust. Our soil was sandy and brown. Where had this car been to be covered in red dust? And why was it hidden in the garage? To conceal the dirt? Surely washing it would have dealt with that problem quickly enough.

"Do you have the keys? For the car?" I asked Lani.

"No. You know how you were asking if anything was missing? I should have said then—mom's handbag was never recovered. She had her cell, wallet, and keys in it. None of it has turned up. The sheriff said they put a trace on her phone, but it must be turned off."

"We're going to have to take the car to search it forensically. I'm sorry. I know this is really hard." I put an arm around Lani's shoulders and squeezed when I noticed the tears in her eyes.

She sniffed and wiped an arm over her face. "No, that's okay. Take it. Do whatever you have to do to catch whoever did this to Mom."

"We'll return it as soon as we're done with it," I promised.

"It's okay. I don't need it. I'll probably end up selling it, anyway."

Pulling out my phone, I dialed my cousin Cameron. He was a mechanic and ran his own garage in Maxxan.

"Cousin Katie, as I live and breathe, what can I do for you this fine day?" he answered.

"Hey Cam, can you tow a car for me? Don't have the keys."

"Uh, yeah, I can. Where is it, and where do I need to take it? Does it need repairs? Cos if so, you're gonna have to wait for that. I'm booked solid for the next week."

"No repairs. I need the tow. We're at Lani's mom's place; it's Mrs. B's car. Need to get it to Grandma's place."

"Cool, I get to check out the renos." I could hear Cameron shuffling papers around, then the sound of a door closing. "On my way now, be there in a few."

Lani and I headed back inside while we waited for the tow truck. I poked around in Mrs. B's home office. Her laptop was here, sitting open on the desk. I powered it up and browsed through her emails when the rumble of Cam's truck disrupted the peace.

"Hey, Lani." Cam jumped down from the cab and enveloped Lani in a bear hug. "So sorry about your mom."

"Thanks, Cam." Lani sniffed, and her eyes filled with tears again.

Steeling my spine against her overwhelming

sadness, I placed a comforting hand on Lani's shoulder. I knew how this felt. I knew what it meant to have your world fall apart so unexpectedly. I also knew that life went on, whether you wanted it to or not. The times I wanted the world to stop turning so I could get off were few and far between these days. But earlier, when the pain of loss was fresh, I'd wanted nothing more than to curl up and die, to join them in Heaven and end my miserable existence on this earth.

We stood and watched as Cam hooked up the back of the car to his truck. He then used a long piece of metal to break into the driver's side door, reached in, popped the gear stick into neutral, and released the handbrake. Reaching into the cab of his truck, he pressed a button, and the tow truck dragged the car out of the garage and slowly up and onto the tray bed. It was done within minutes, and Cameron was standing in front of me, squinting into the sun, sweat darkening his coveralls.

"Meet you out there?" he said, tugging the brim of his baseball cap lower.

"Sure. And keep this on the down-low, will you? I'll pay you, of course, but if you can keep it off the books, that'd be great."

He joked over his shoulder as he walked away,

"Sounds shady, but for you, I'll make an exception. But only 'cos you're family."

"Lani," I began, but she interrupted me before I could finish.

"I won't say anything. That you were here, that you took Mom's car. I get it. You don't want to tip off whoever did this. Which means you think they're still in Maxxan, that this wasn't some random psychopath passing through town."

She was right, in a sense. Her mom wasn't killed by a random person passing through town, but there was no way I could tell her a ghoul ate her mom. There's only so much a girl can take, and I doubted very much that Lani's mental health could take such a hit. It was up to the SIA to get to the bottom of this, catch the ghouls—hell, catch Ridgeway, and end this craziness once and for all. If only I knew where to look to find the psychopath in question.

THIRTEEN

I was gathering dirt samples from Mrs. B's car when Rae burst into the garage slash workshop. "Oh my God, I saw her, I'm sure of it!"

"Saw who?" I asked. "And don't touch the car! It's evidence."

"The Red Witch!"

I paused from where I was crouched at the front bumper and glanced at her. She was positively vibrating with energy. And if it was true, if she had seen the Red Witch, then it was entirely possible the vampire attack we'd been called out to by the sheriff had indeed been the Gunslinger.

"Where?" Keeping my voice neutral, I slowly straightened and removed my gloves with a snap.

Rae was wired as it was; I didn't need her rushing off and doing anything foolish. She was new to the SIA, and I made myself remember how exciting it was to get your first break on a case.

"This shop in town. I was walking past and caught a glimpse of red hair in the window as I went by, so I backtracked and peeked inside. I'm sure it was her, Katie."

"Okay, okay. What shop?"

"One of those new-age hippy ones. It looked like she was buying candles."

"So, a place, you'd think, where a witch might purchase supplies?" I hinted, and Rae snapped her fingers and pointed at me, "Yes! Of course."

"And what do you think we should do about it?" It was a question I'd ask any recruit in training, and Rae was no different.

"Go and arrest her, of course." She nodded, pleased with herself.

"Before that?" Tossing my gloves into the bin, I unzipped the disposable coveralls that made my skin itch and threw them in the bin, too. I had six samples from different areas of the car to send to the lab. Unfortunately, the lab was in Redmeadows, so I'd have to wait for the results, but I'd finally found a thread I could tug on. The lab should be able to tell us what area the dust and dirt particles came from.

"Oh. Ummm."

I waited while Rae thought about her next plan of action. The Red Witch and the Gunslinger were on the SIA's most-wanted list. They were dangerous. I had to make sure this was done right, and that Rae didn't go charging in and putting herself in jeopardy.

"First of all, you want to find out if the shop owner—or whoever served her—remembers her coming in. Take a photo with you. Ask if she paid by cash or credit card," I prompted.

"If she paid by card, get a copy of the transaction."

"And then?"

"Ask if they can tell us anything more about her. Was she alone? Which way did she go when she left? What did she say?"

"Excellent. Right, let's go."

"You're coming with me?" Her pout was adorable, and I knew exactly what she was thinking. That she was a badass Shelton woman who didn't need help. With anything. I often had similar feelings myself.

"You bet your ass I'm coming. I'm not letting you

walk into danger alone. You remember the Red Witch, right? You were face to face with her, and if she's in town and recognizes you? Don't think she's going to walk on over and say, 'Hi, nice to see you again.' She's going to kick your ass. And I won't have that."

"I hate it when you're right." She softened the words with a face-splitting grin, then patted her weapon, mentally going through what she'd been taught. I waited.

"Pyre gun, check," she whispered to herself, "restraining cuff, check. Bear, check—wait, where's Bear?" Opening the garage door, she spied her hellhound asleep under a tree, his snore blowing up dust.

"Ready?" I asked, stepping around her and out into the blistering heat. SIA had coughed up enough cash to have all the buildings air-conditioned, and while I genuinely loved the heat, it was nice to work without sweat dripping in your eyes.

"We taking the nark mobile?" she asked, cocking her head at one of our larger vehicles that had a cage in the back for restraining and transporting paranormals.

"Of course. Suppose we catch up with her in town? In that case, we'll need to bring her in, so we have to go prepared, and with the dampening effect of the cage and the restraining collar, she won't be able to use her magic to escape." I hoped. The Red Witch was one of the most powerful witches the SIA had encountered; the reality was I had no idea if our pyre guns would work on her or if the restraining collar would be sufficient. When placed around a paranormal's neck, the collar locked down their supernatural abilities. So shifters couldn't shift, vampires were weakened, and witches couldn't use magic.

"Here," I tossed her the keys, "you drive." I planned to pack up my samples on the way into town, then post them to HQ.

We stopped at the post office first, then proceeded down Main Street to the shop where Rae had seen the Red Witch. The sign on the window read Black Magic, and I raised a brow at Rae. "Seriously?"

She shrugged. "I know, right?"

I indicated she should lead the way and followed her inside. It was dim in the shop, and it smelled weird. Not an incense-type smell, something else, something more...potent. It was so potent it made the hairs on my arms stand on end. I let Rae approach the counter and talk to the clerk while I perused the shelves, my senses going haywire. Could Rae feel it? I watched through a shelf full of candles, keeping an eye on her, but she was chatting to the young man behind the counter, his hair twisted into a man bun, his face half-hidden by a beard. She seemed relaxed enough, hyped up with excitement. Still, she was being professional, showing him the photo of the Red Witch on her phone. He leaned forward and studied the picture for a second or two before shaking his head. *Liar.* I could feel something in this shop, and whatever it was, I'd bet it was connected with the Red Witch.

Rae slid her phone back into her pocket and thanked the young man with a smile before making her way over to me.

"Nope, he says he hasn't seen her."

"And do you believe him?" I asked.

"Not in the slightest." She gave me a shit-eating grin, and I was so proud of her at that moment. She was going to make an excellent SIA Agent.

"This is black magic occult." I pointed to a dagger on the shelf I was standing next to. "This is dark stuff. She was here."

"So, what now? We stake out the joint? Wait for her to return?" Rae asked, but I was already shaking my head.

"She's already bought her supplies. And this guy, who'd remember a sizzling hot redhead, I'm sure, will most likely alert her that we've been in asking questions as soon as we leave."

"What then?"

"We're at an impasse. We're relatively sure she's in town, which means so is the Gunslinger, but we have nothing concrete to confirm that. So, we need to go hunting. Let's get back to SIA, and we'll head out from there. I want to bring Jordan in on this."

Rae talked the entire drive back to our new offices, and by the time we arrived, we'd hit on a plan. She and Jordan knew where the Red Witch had been trapped before they'd freed her and discovered she was one of the bad guys. It was an old abandoned farm, and she'd been chained in an underground storage room carved from stone beneath the barn. Her scent would be all over it, and all we had to do was get Bear on the job.

Faithful hellhound that he was, he'd followed us all the way into Maxxan and back again and wasn't even panting. It was a fun afternoon run for him.

The sun was low on the horizon, and my stomach was growling when we pulled up. I'd skipped lunch, and it had been a long time since breakfast.

"You got food here?" I asked Rae. Since I'd bailed on staying at the offices and was now set up in Paige's apartment in town, I hadn't thought to restock the pantry here.

"Jordan took care of it," Rae answered, swiping her card and unlocking the front door. "If it were me, we'd probably be having frozen pizza for dinner. That man is my savior."

"You got eggs?" I already knew the answer. Rae would have no clue what food items were in the fridge. Cooking was not her forte. Nor was it Paige's. It seemed I was the only Shelton woman who had inherited any cooking DNA. "Don't answer that. I'll check for myself."

Continuing down the hallway to the kitchen, I flung open the refrigerator and smiled—fully stocked. And I mean fully. Fresh veggies, milk, butter, eggs, juice. Even a cheesecake hid at the back, unopened.

"You want an omelet?" I called out. Rae had veered off into the open plan workstation area, and her muffled reply of, "Does a bear shit in the woods?" had me laughing. Rae would eat anything I put in front of her, whether she was hungry or not. I was preparing the omelets when I heard the lock on the front door beep and heavy boots down the hallway. Jordan and Brax were back. I doubled the omelet mix without asking.

"Hey." Just the sound of his voice was enough to make me shiver in anticipation.

"Hey," I replied, glancing at Brax, where he lounged against the doorframe. "How did it go?"

"Stonewalled. You?"

"Actually, made some progress today." I couldn't contain the relief in my voice. Our investigation had stalled. We were losing time, and I'd been worried Nate was going to take me off as the lead. This investigation was good for my career, and I needed to make it work. I filled him in about Mrs. B's car and that Rae had seen the Red Witch in town, and our progress on both.

"You're kicking my ass, Shelton," he teased. "I'm not sure I like it."

"Pft, SIA will always trump Secret Service," I drawled, serving up an omelet and handing the plate to him. "Here. Eat. We've got more work to do tonight; you'll need your strength."

"I love it when a woman says that." He winked and was gone. I heard him tell the others that the food was ready, and I swear it was like, two seconds later, both Rae and Jordan were in the doorway, faces expectant.

"Yeah, yeah, give me a second. I can only cook one at a time. Seriously, it's like you two haven't eaten in a week."

"It's only because we've experienced your extraordinary culinary skills and know that what to us mere mortals is simply an omelet. From you, it is nirvana," Jordan told me, laying the praise on so thick I'd need a shovel to get it off.

"You win!" I handed him the next omelet while Rae slapped him on the ass.

"No fair, that's cheating. I can't butter her up like that. We grew up together—she'd know I was lying."

"Careful," I warned. "Don't make me spit in yours."

After we'd all eaten, I outlined the plan. We'd travel in pairs out to the old farmhouse; Bear would pick up the scent and lead us to the Red Witch. It sounded simple on paper. Easy. Of course, nothing about hunting the Red Witch would be easy.

"What weapons do you have, Brax? You guys have pyres?" The SIA-issued pyre guns could be set to stun or kill, and I wanted the Red Witch alive.

"I've got an ankle holster fully loaded, and yeah, we have pyres." He unlocked his desk drawer and withdrew a gun belt. "Don't have that restraining collar, though." He nodded toward Jordan, whose collar was clipped to the side of his belt.

"Jordan, grab one for him, would you? Actually, let's go fully loaded. She won't be alone; we just might find our cells at full capacity tonight."

FOURTEEN

Rae jumped from the cab of her truck and whistled for Bear as we pulled up at the farmhouse. It had taken us two hours to drive out here—to the ass-end of nowhere. No wonder this place was deserted. How anyone had managed to survive out here, let alone run a farm, was beyond me.

The old barn had been blown apart, but the cellar beneath was still there, and Jordan tossed debris aside to allow Bear access. I couldn't contain the chuckle at the sight of Bear trying to fit through the narrow doorway; it simply wasn't going to happen. Instead, he stuck his head inside, and we could hear him sniffing and snorting as he dragged in the scents.

"How will he know which scent to follow?" I asked Rae.

She stood with her arms folded across her chest, legs planted, patiently waiting. "You know, I don't know exactly how it works," she began, "but it's like Bear knows what I want. Like he understands me. Maybe he does; maybe he understands English but can't speak. Or we have some strange connection because ever since he chose me, no matter where I am, he can find me."

With a loud snort, Bear pulled his head out and shook, dust flying from his fur, forcing us to raise our arms to shield ourselves from the sandstorm he unexpectedly unleashed.

"You got it, Bear?" Rae asked, rubbing her hand up and down the giant dog's snout. "Can you find the witch, baby? Take me to her?"

Bear barked, and the ground trembled beneath our feet. "Good boy," Rae cooed. "Let me up, and we'll go get her." Bear lay down and let Rae climb onto his back, her fingers gripping his fur tightly. He was bigger than any horse, and she looked ridiculously small on his back.

"Hold on. I'm coming with you." Jordan vaulted up behind Rae, wrapping his arms around her waist.

"Shit! They're going to be fast. Turn your

trackers on!" I yelled, sprinting for my truck, Brax one step ahead of me. Bear was off and running before I'd even turned the key in the ignition. Slamming the car into gear, I peeled after him, dirt and rocks flicking up from the spinning tires. Fishtailing down the dirt road, I peered ahead, trying to keep my eyes on the dust cloud that was Bear, but it was impossible. Night had fallen, and I could only see so far, even with the spotlight mounted on the front of the truck.

Brax punched in something on the GPS. "I've got them," he told me, and I switched my attention from trying to physically see Bear to following the red dot that appeared on the GPS. All of us wore trackers; they were implanted in the watches on our wrists, but for privacy, we only activated them when on a mission.

The drive was wild. Veering off the road, I threw the truck into four-wheel drive and bounced over abandoned fields, through a disused quarry, back onto an unpaved road, and off again. My teeth rattled in my head from the jarring, but I daren't slow the pace. Jordan and Rae would need backup. Brax was holding on to the door, his eyes intent on the GPS, giving me verbal directions since I needed all my attention to control the vehicle.

"They've stopped," he told me, "Not far ahead. Slow down and turn off your lights."

I did as instructed, casting a glance at the GPS. He was right; the red dot was no longer moving. Looking around, I tried to work out where we were —another abandoned farm? We bounced over a large embankment and onto a paved road.

"Oh my God," I whispered as we slowly made our way forward, "this is the Everly Plantation."

"Deserted?" Brax asked, but I was already shaking my head. "No. No, it isn't."

I killed the engine and coasted to a stop when the gates to the property came into view. "The Everly Plantation produces a unique rum; it's world-famous," I explained, "And now I'm really curious why the Red Witch is here. Could she be helping with the crops? Some sort of spell to ensure they keep producing?"

"Could be. Or it could be something totally innocent," Brax pointed out, and my head swiveled so fast I almost cricked my neck. He chuckled. "Okay, okay, I take that back. I'm sure it's not innocent. We were expecting some run-down, abandoned place where they wouldn't be discovered. Instead, we discover she's here, at a rum distillery, doing who knows what. Maybe she's purchasing supplies?"

"Only one way to find out." I'd spotted Jordan and Rae waiting on the inside of the gate. Bear flopped down in the shadows, head on his paws, taking a nap. Opening the door, I made my way over to them, Brax right behind me.

"What do you think?" Jordan asked me.

"To be honest, it's taken me by surprise," I admitted. "This changes things. There are civilians here. Let's get closer, scout it out, then work out a plan of action. I want to know what she's doing here. Check your coms; report in if you see her."

We split up and made our way up the long, winding driveway, the tall trees providing extra shelter from prying eyes. The Everly Plantation had been built over a hundred years ago. As far as I knew, it was still owned by the original family. The big old mansion ahead of us housed living quarters, offices, and a restaurant. It loomed majestically at the end of a circular drive, three stories high, with tall white columns running along the front of the building. Strategic lighting showcased the plantation mansion in all its glory—the rum business was booming, judging by the manicured gardens and five-star, exclusive restaurant with high-end cars parked in the lot.

Jordan and Rae were approaching from the front, Brax and I from the rear. Ducking down the side of the building, I crouched low and kept to the shadows when a beam of red light caught my attention. I froze, crouching to examine it. A tripwire of sorts. Using my coms, I whispered into the device on my wrist, "Use caution—they've got motion sensors." Stepping over it, I continued until I reached the corner. I plastered myself against the side of the building and cautiously peered around the corner. It was darker here. Keeping low, I darted forward. There was a back porch, partially enclosed, and several outbuildings. About a hundred yards further back was another building, huge, with a single bulb above the door. I decided to check it out. "Brax. You check the house. I'm checking the distillery," I said into my coms unit.

"Affirmative," he replied into my earpiece.

Darting across the yard, I weaved around plants and shrubs, keeping an eye out for any more motion detectors. When I reached the building, I crept up and pressed myself against the brick surface, inching along until I came to a window. Standing on tiptoes, I peered inside, seeing six massive steel tanks. This must be the distillery. I was about to leave, not expecting to find anything here, when the sound of voices had me freezing in my tracks. Holding my breath, I strained to listen but couldn't make out what they were saying. It definitely sounded like a man and a woman, though. I seriously doubted the Red Witch would be hanging out in the rum distillery, but since I was here, I might as well check it out. Didn't hurt to be thorough.

There was too much light at the front of the building to gain entry undetected, so I quickly moved to the rear of the building, sticking my head around first. It was dark and deserted, which was perfect, but less than perfect was the fact that there was no door. Hurrying along the back, I quickly looked down the other side of the building and breathed a sigh of relief. Yes, a side door. Approaching it, I glanced around to make sure I was alone. I couldn't sense anyone; crickets were chirping, so I had no reason to believe I had been spotted. It, therefore, came as a big surprise to feel something hard pressed between my shoulder blades and a deep voice say, "Don't move."

I froze. My pyre gun was removed from its

holster, and I cursed. How had I missed this? How had I not heard him approaching?

"Hands up. No sudden moves." I raised my hands, already plotting how I was going to get out of this. As far as I could tell, it was just him and me. Once that gun was removed from my back, I'd have one brief moment of opportunity to take him down. Poking me again, he ordered, "Move," and pushed me toward the door. I stumbled forward, waited while he reached around me to punch in a code, and that's when I struck. The gun was still at my back, but it was worth the risk. He was distracted with the alarm pad, and despite wanting to see what was beyond the door, I didn't want to do it at such a distinct disadvantage.

Simultaneously grabbing his wrist while elbowing him in the gut, I bent forward, effectively forcing him to lie over my back. I rolled him over me in slow motion until he fell to the ground in front of me. My strength had been the element of surprise. Seizing my pyre gun that he'd tucked into his waistband, I fired, and his body went rigid before slumping into unconsciousness. Grabbing one of the collars from my belt, I snapped it around his neck, then dragged him clear of the doorway. While we'd scuffled, the door had clicked open and now stood slightly ajar. I checked on him, pressing my fingers against his neck. His pulse was strong. I wasn't sure what type of paranormal he was, but the stun from the pyre gun would keep him out for a while, and he wouldn't be able to get the collar off when he woke up, but that didn't mean I wanted him running around alerting others. I pulled zip ties from my pocket and secured him to a nearby drainpipe before creeping into the distillery.

"Finally," a female voice drawled, and I froze, eyes darting from side to side but seeing nothing.

"Come out!" I ordered, pyre gun held between both hands, scanning, searching for movement.

"Lower your gun first."

Slowly I lowered my gun, aiming it at the floor but keeping a firm grip on it. I'd been caught off guard once; I wasn't about to let it happen again. A woman stepped out from behind one of the massive steel vats. Her flaming red hair gave her away. "The Red Witch, I assume."

"At your service," she replied, stepping forward. I watched her warily. Although I couldn't see or hear anyone else, I knew she wasn't alone. Moments before, she'd been talking to someone. There hadn't been enough time for him to leave, which meant he was here, watching, waiting.

"What are you doing here?" I demanded, glancing around, trying to pinpoint where the other person was.

"Waiting for you." Crossing her arms over her chest, she moved her weight to one leg and eyed me up and down. "It's come to my attention that we have a mutual goal."

"Oh?" Feeling exposed, I moved toward her, fingers gripping the pyre gun so tight my knuckles shone white. I stopped when my back was to the tank.

"There's a pesky shifter that needs taking care of." She nodded, examining her nails.

"You want the SIA to take care of a shifter problem you're having?" I couldn't believe the gall of her.

She laughed. "Oh, my dear, she's your problem, too. You might recognize the name—Ridgeway?"

"You're after Keri Ridgeway?" I scoffed. "What did she do, double-cross you?"

"Oh, we aren't working together." She flicked a piece of invisible lint from her leather pants. "Never have been. But we've been aware of her little experiments for some time now. Really didn't think anything would come of it, to be honest, and who am I to stop a fellow psychopath?"

It was disconcerting to hear her refer to herself as a psychopath, but what had my attention was the fact that she wasn't working with Ridgeway.

She laughed again. "Your face is priceless. And as transparent as glass."

"What the fuck is going on? What are you talking about?" Anger colored my words, anger because while her henchman had caught me off guard outside, now she was catching me off guard with her words.

"I am saying Ridgeway has become a problem, and I want her stopped."

"And?"

"And from what I hear, you want the same thing. I propose we work together."

I made a sound between a snort and a laugh. "You've got to be kidding me. You're on the SIA's most-wanted list. I can't work with you, but I can take you in." I raised my gun and aimed it at her chest, my finger resting on the trigger.

"You Shelton women are such little hellcats," a dark, seductive voice drawled right by my ear. My finger squeezed the trigger in response, and the gun fired. Only the Red Witch was no longer standing in front of me. She was leaning on the vat next to mine, playing with a strand of hair. I slowly turned my head to the man by my side, the one I knew had been in the building somewhere, only I'd had no sense of him. Now I knew who it was, the dark good looks, the porn star mustache, the boots, the long coat, the cowboy hat.

"Gunslinger," I breathed, my breath hitching in my throat when he ran his hand down my arm and gently forced me to lower my gun.

"At your service, sweetheart," he drawled. And then the bastard bit me.

FIFTEEN

The bite had been quick but thorough. I'd felt the sting as his fangs had sunk into my artery, the long pull as he consumed my blood. Then he stepped back, his lips curled in a self-satisfied smirk as he ran his tongue over his bottom lip, removing the last remaining trace of my blood.

"That's rude!" Slapping a hand over my bleeding neck, I frowned at him, annoyed beyond belief that these two had gotten the better of me.

He laughed, incensing me further. "Just heal yourself," he said, "although,"—he breathed in deeply through his nose—"The smell of your blood is almost as intoxicating as the taste, so on second thought, stand there and bleed, little one."

Pressing my fingers tighter against my neck, I tried to stem the bleeding, feeling the warm wetness as it squeezed between my fingers. Flaming to heal myself was not an option. For one, my clothes would burn, and I sure as hell wasn't going to be running around the Everly Plantation naked, and two, we were standing in a distillery. We'd all go up in flames. I narrowed my eyes, considering that option. Did the Red Witch have the skills to save them both from a massive fireball?

"Tsk." The Red Witch waved her hand at me, and I felt the flesh of my neck knead back together. "Don't you know anything?" She turned her annoyance on the Gunslinger.

"What?" the Gunslinger drawled, seemingly amused by the whole thing.

"She's a fire demon, and we're surrounded by a flammable liquid." I could practically hear the word *idiot* tacked on the end. My gaze darted between the two of them—they had interesting chemistry. Rae had reported that they had been romantically involved, once, but then he'd trapped her in the cellar after she'd spelled Maxxan to allow vampires to walk in the sun. After Rae and Jordan had accidentally released her, she'd lifted the curse, and she and the Gunslinger had been arguing ever since.

While they bickered, I slowly moved my hand and pressed the silent alarm on my wrist unit. Immediately Brax's voice was in my ear. "On my way." Good, that was good. Despite the Gunslinger's bite being fast, I was swaying on my feet. He'd drained a lot of blood in a short amount of time, and I was starting to feel the wobbly effects.

"What are you two doing here?" I demanded, drawing their attention back to me. "Last I heard, you hightailed out of here when the SIA busted your drug ring."

The Gunslinger threw back his head and laughed, long and loud, and even the Red Witch had a chuckle.

"Why are you laughing? This isn't funny. I'm serious." This only made the Red Witch laugh more, and irritation had blue electricity sparks running along my skin. My fingers curled into fists as I tried to rein in my power. As much as I'd dearly love to pitch a fireball at her, I was pretty sure the owners of the Everly Plantation would not be pleased with me torching their money-making distillery.

"Caution." The Gunslinger was suddenly in front of me, moving so fast I couldn't track his movements, his hand closing around my clenched fist. "As tempting as it is to barbecue us all, I wouldn't advise it."

I snatched my hand away and stepped sideways, avoiding his touch. The Gunslinger was a handsome man and exuded a charm that was both old-worldly and intoxicating. I was also reasonably sure that he used it to his advantage as often as possible. Still, despite his sparkling blue eyes and engaging smile, I wasn't moved. My pulse didn't accelerate, and I didn't feel the need to bat my lashes at him.

"Interesting." He followed. For each step back I made, he stepped forward until he grew impatient with our game and shot a hand around the nape of my neck to halt my backward trajectory. I filled my lungs with air, held it for several seconds before slowly releasing it, steadying my nerves, giving myself time to think, and time—I hoped—for Brax to reach me.

"What is?" I didn't want to buy into his game, but I did need to buy myself time, and if engaging him in inane banter was the way to do it, then that was precisely what I would do.

"Your essence." He breathed in deeply again and pushed his face against my hair, and I froze. He was a dangerous man, a powerful vampire who'd outsmarted Jordan once; I'd be wise to remember that. "I've tasted it before."

"What?" the Red Witch and I said in unison. I'd never met him in person before; there was no way he could have "tasted" my essence. Whatever that meant.

"Is she the one?" The Red Witch approached with long, slinky strides, hips swaying, her seductive aura filling the surrounding air. That's when it hit me. It was the two of them together, creating a sensual atmosphere. Not his flirting. They were feeding off each other and emitted something into the air. Cocking my head, I studied them, wondering if they were fated mates. They had the classic off-the-charts chemistry that made you think of lust and sex and very little else.

"The one what?" I asked, my patience running out. They talked in riddles, exuded distracting pheromones into the air when all I wanted was answers to my questions. Oh, and for them to surrender, preferably quietly.

"Where's the child?" The Red Witch grabbed my chin, her fingers pinching, and I winced.

"What child?" I was confused. What kid were they talking about? Surely not Abigail? She'd been a baby when she'd died—and how would they even know of her existence? A headache was starting to pound at my temples, and I squinted my eyes while I jerked my chin out of her grip.

Letting me go, she grabbed The Gunslinger's arm. Clutching at it with both hands, she looked up into his face. "It's her, isn't it?" she breathed, her voice giving away her excitement. "It has to be. She's a fire demon. And a Shelton. She's the one Ridgeway is searching for."

"I am beginning to think you are right," the Gunslinger replied, dropping a kiss on the Red Witch's nose. She beamed at him, then slapped his ass, the action taking me by surprise and making me jump.

"Freeze! Hands in the air, we've got you surrounded!" Brax's shout had me sagging in relief. I watched as he made his way into the distillery, a gun in each hand, Rae and Jordan flanking him, weapons drawn.

"Cavalry's here." The Gunslinger smiled at the Red Witch as they both turned to face Brax, hands raised. This was too easy, I realized. It was like they'd been waiting, toying with me while waiting for the others to arrive.

"Brax," I warned, "I have a feeling this is a trap."

"Smart as well as beautiful," the Gunslinger said.

"Get over here, Katie," Brax ordered. "Are you hurt?" His eyes lingered on the dried blood on my neck, but I shook my head.

"I'm fine."

"He bit you?" As soon as I was within arm's reach, he lifted his hand to touch the healed skin on my throat. Without giving me a chance to answer, Brax fired. I gasped, swinging around to watch, expecting to see the Gunslinger falling. Instead, he stood with hands-on-hips, looking highly amused. The Red Witch had erected a force field around them; I could see it shimmering in the air.

"We only want her." The Red Witch pointed at me. "The rest of you can go, unharmed."

"No deal," Brax spat, shoving me behind him.

"Hey!" I protested, stepping out from behind him. "I can fight my own battles, thank you very much. I don't need you going all alpha male."

"You didn't even have your gun ready," he pointed out. "So clearly, you do need someone looking out for you."

"Guys," Jordan warned.

I ignored him. "You've just seen for yourself how ineffective a weapon is against them," I pointed out, and he had the grace to look at his gun and then back at my face and give a slight nod. We had three fire demons and one dragon against two powerful supernaturals. We could win this. But not in the distillery.

"They lured us here on purpose," I breathed, having a lightbulb moment. "They know we won't risk blowing this place sky high, that we won't use our fire against them."

"Yeah, well, that's where they misjudged us," Jordan spat, "because I don't care about protecting some human property. They have insurance. They can rebuild." With that, he transformed into his dragon, and he was as massive as he was magnificent.

"Oh my," the Gunslinger murmured, "now that is impressive."

Jordan extended his wings, and they crashed through the roof, raining debris down on us. Arms over my head, I ran toward a vat and huddled against it, Brax in front of me, shielding me. Rae followed his lead, lighting up her palms with fireballs and tossing them at the Red Witch and Gunslinger. Each hit was weakening the force field surrounding them; each fireball protruded that bit farther. I saw the worried glance between the two of them. They hadn't been expecting us to fight.

"Come on." I pushed Brax in the back. "Let's get the bastards. Fire!" Running forward, I summoned my fireballs and began hurling them at the shield, Brax by my side. I grinned triumphantly. With the four of us bombarding them with fire, we'd win, I was sure of it.

The next thing I knew, I was underwater, and it was pitch black. Where the hell was I? And where was Brax? I blinked, and my eyes burned as if acid was eating at my eyeballs. I let out a gurgled scream, precious oxygen leeching from my lungs while I screwed up my eyes to stop any more of the toxic liquid from getting in. Legs kicking, I swam, trying to find the surface, only there was no surface. My fingers met the cold steel of a distillery vat, and that's when I realized the Red Witch had transported me inside. I was inside a tank of rum. There was no air, no light, and very little hope of getting out of here alive. I banged on the roof of the vat and felt around for a hatch or opening of some sort, even an air pocket, but it was sealed tight.

I could hear voices outside, shouting, and hands banging on the vat wall. I beat in return. *Help! Get me out!* My lungs were burning, and I knew I wouldn't be able to hold back from dragging in a lungful of rum at any second. My skin hurt from the alcohol, my limbs struggled with the heavy weight of my clothes, and finally, I gulped in a breath of rum before coughing and choking. Then I was floating, coughs still wracking me as my lungs filled up with the burning rum. Then it didn't burn anymore. I felt lightheaded, and I knew I was dying. I hadn't been expecting to die today, but one thought comforted me—I'd see my baby girl soon. I was on my way. With one last gurgle, I stopped breathing. *I'm coming, Abigail; Momma's coming.*

SIXTEEN

The heat was unrelenting, as were the flames consuming me. I burned from the inside out. Time no longer had meaning, and I wondered if I was in Hell, for this was how I'd imagine it to be, a never-ending fire that consumed your soul, leaving you broken and hollow, never to survive outside the flame, always a prisoner. For eternity.

"Come on, Shelton, snap out of it." I was startled at Brax's voice growling in my ear, a distinct note of annoyance in his words. But now I was confused. Brax was in Hell too?

A sharp sting on my cheek had my head snapping back, and my eyes flew open. Brax stood in front of me, ablaze with his flame, hands-on-hips. I raised my hand to my cheek, realized I was flaming too. Healing.

"You hit me!" The sting had been him slapping me. Without even thinking about it, a fireball formed in my hand. No one slapped me and got away with it.

"Settle down. You were out of it. Now you're not. It worked. You're welcome." He recalled his flame and stood naked before me. I didn't look away. Couldn't, because he was magnificent in all his natural glory. A surge of lust flooded my system, pounded through my veins with every beat of my heart, sizzled so hot my toes curled. I recalled my flame by reflex and knew he could see me, naked and vulnerable, by how his eyes darkened with passion.

Cautiously, as if I might flee, he stepped closer, his hand reaching out until his fingers traced the skin over my shoulder. "You're healed." It wasn't said with wonder or reverence, merely stating a fact. As fire demons, we could set ourselves on fire and heal ourselves. But I hadn't, not ever. I bore the scars of childbirth, the faint stretch marks that I cherished. And the wound on my shoulder from the car accident. The SIA had wanted me to heal, to be fully functional, but I'd refused. My shoulder was good enough. If I flamed, I'd erase the last traces of Abigail. And now that very thing had happened. To survive, to live, I had to flame. Only I didn't remember doing it. All I remembered was drowning in a vat of rum.

My desire faded as I recalled recent events, and I stepped back, crossing my arms over my chest, hiding my breasts from his view. I couldn't process the fact that my body was perfect, that I'd flamed and decimated my last connection to my daughter, so I focused on the only thing I could.

"Where are they?" I demanded. He knew who I was referring to, of course, for we were still in the distillery. Half the roof was missing, and a vat was raging with a fire that was fast consuming the building. Yet, I had no urge to flee, and I wondered if I was brain-damaged from marinating in the alcohol.

"They've gone. Rae and Jordan are pursuing them. And now we need to get out of here. The humans are coming, and we don't need to be answering questions as to why we're standing buck naked in their burning distillery."

"But what happened? I died. I didn't flame." I could hear voices now, shouting, and Brax shook his head, shoving me toward the door.

"Move."

I went. He was right. I didn't want to be caught, and I especially didn't want to be caught naked. We dashed outside and ran, keeping to the trees. Our vehicle was near the gates of the Everly Plantation, which was on the other side of the property, which meant a long trek back without being seen. Thankfully, the blazing distillery provided a brilliant distraction. Only I felt like crap that we'd set it on fire. I stepped on something sharp and stopped, hobbling to lean on a tree as I pulled a sharp twig from the sole of my foot. Brax stopped and backtracked, leaning on the other side of the tree. In the shadows, I listened to our ragged breathing as we caught our breath.

"The Red Witch teleported you into a vat." Brax's voice was so low I had to strain to hear. "And I figured you probably panicked, inhaled the rum, and were soon incapacitated. Jordan had already shifted into his dragon and totaled the roof. We weren't going to be able to keep our presence secret, so I flamed for you."

"But how did you get to me?" I hadn't been able to get out of the vat. How had he gotten in?

"I opened the hatch, reached in, hauled you out, and flamed. Of course, that created a massive fireball that blew the sides of the vat open, and burning alcohol went everywhere. The distillery is fucked."

I blew out a breath, relishing the rush of air in my lungs, the reminder of rum in my airways an unpleasant memory. "I feel bad about that. Our number one objective is to keep the humans unaware of our presence. We blew up their distillery."

"Jordan is taking care of it." Brax moved, and the leaves beneath his feet crackled, the sound loud in the night air. "He's making it look like a freak windstorm came through. With that wingspan of his, it only took two seconds."

I digested what he'd told me. Jordan had made it all look like a random act of nature. A very unfortunate one, but better than the alternative of revealing to the humans who we truly are.

"Let's go." I needed time to think, regroup, and examine everything that had happened here tonight, but that was hard to do with a fire raging behind us and sneaking around naked in the grounds of Everly Plantation. Brax led the way. Normally I'd bristle at him taking the lead, but tonight I was content to follow. Maybe I'd pickled some brain cells in the vat. Or perhaps it was because I enjoyed the view of his naked ass, what I could see of it in the dim light. Now and then, moonlight filtered through and splayed a dappled pattern across his shoulders and back, and I'd bite my lip to stop from tracing my fingers over his flesh.

"What are you doing?" He'd stopped, and I ran smack bang into the back of him, my breasts flattening against his back, and I felt him go rigid.

"What?" I squeaked, not unaffected by the sudden full-body contact.

He didn't reply, and long moments passed. Neither of us moved, and I closed my eyes, resting my cheek against his back, breathing in the scent of him. My arms were limp by my sides, and I didn't protest when his hand reached for mine and our fingers entwined. This was life. This was worth flaming for, and it was a revelation, a stunning, terrifying revelation. I had feelings. Feelings for Brax that I swore I'd never have.

"You'd better not be crying," he growled, making me jump.

My head snapped up, and I realized I was, in fact, crying. I wasn't sure why, so I quickly wiped the tears away and lied. "No." Then I noticed the glistening trail of tears on his bare skin where my face had rested and quickly wiped away the evidence. "My eyes still sting from the vat."

He didn't reply but began walking again, keeping a tight hold on my hand. There was no time to be distracted by his magnificent body as we reached the main building and all its floodlit glory. We had to get around the front and down the driveway without being detected. It had seemed easier fully clothed, our black uniform offering not only protection but camouflage. I felt like my white skin was glowing neon in the darkness, a sure-fire "come find me" beacon to anyone who happened to glance outside. Stopping, Brax turned to me, releasing my hand to cup my face.

"Ready?" he whispered.

"No. I'm feeling..." I didn't know what I was feeling. Different. Strange. All marshmallowy inside, and I didn't know how to deal with it. While we weren't exactly in a life-or-death situation right this second, we were in a perilous one, and I needed to get my head back in the game. *Except. Brax. Naked.* Lips so close, all I had to do was lean forward and taste them.

"Your timing sucks, Katie Shelton." He dropped a hard kiss on my lips, swiveled, and pulled me behind him as he sprinted from shadow to shadow, pressing our unprotected skin up against the buildings as we made our way forward. I didn't feel the scrapes, didn't feel the bite of pebbles underfoot that should have made me wince.

"Brax!" I skidded to a halt, panic flooding me.

He immediately spun, looking over my head for a threat. Finding none, his eyes met mine. "What is it?"

"Something's wrong with me," I whispered, my eyes revealing my distress.

"You're hurt?" His eyes immediately raked over my body, searching for signs of injury, but I was shaking my head.

"No. Not like that. Why can't I focus?"

"You can't see?" He peered closer, his face inches from mine. I couldn't stand it. I launched at him, wrapping my arms around his neck and kissing him. His hands settled on my hips, and his mouth opened, his tongue meeting mine in the most delicious caress. I felt the crackle of electricity dance over my skin, my passion unguarded.

"I can't believe I'm going to say this." He wrenched his mouth away, and I gripped his hair, tugging his head back to me. "But you need to rein it in, Katie. You're going to get us caught. You're sparking all over the place; someone is going to see."

His words were a bucket of cold water. I released him immediately and jumped back, turning so he couldn't see my face and the heat burning there. I wanted him so badly I could barely think. I wanted to consume him and make him mine, regardless of the fact that we were skulking around nude in the middle of the night after blowing up a distillery. This was dangerous. He was dangerous. Which only made me crave him more. It was as if a floodgate had opened, and everything that I'd kept buried had burst forth, unbidden and uncontrolled and feral.

"Hey." He turned me back to face him. "I'm not saying no. I'm saying not right now, for as much as I want to push you up against this wall—now is not the time. But hold that thought. I'm getting us out of here as quickly as I can, believe me."

I nodded, my mind a riot of doubt, lust, and confusion. I had no idea what was happening to me. All I could do was ride it out and pray this molten need didn't consume me first.

SEVENTEEN

"Put this on." I caught the T-shirt Brax tossed at me and obediently pulled it over my head. It reached my thighs, and while it covered everything essential, by the way Brax's eyes devoured me, it didn't help, not really. Climbing into the passenger seat, I waited. He rummaged around in the back of the SUV and finally opened the driver's side door and slid in. I cast him a glance and snorted when all he had on was a small towel strategically draped over his lap.

"What?" he asked, starting the engine.

"Just wondering where you were keeping those keys." I grinned.

He arched a brow and winked. "Someplace safe."

I laughed, then turned my attention to the

windscreen. Flames still leaped into the sky, where the fire continued to rage. With all the rum to fuel it, I'd imagine it would take them some time to gain control, and again I felt bad for what we'd done.

"Don't," Brax told me.

"How are you reading my mind?" I said defensively, crossing my arms over my chest and forcing the hem of the T-shirt to ride up.

"Because I know you. And you're beating yourself up that we started that fire. I'll look into it and make sure they have the appropriate insurance, and if they don't, we'll make it happen. The Secret Service has its perks. Now do me a favor and cover up, will you?"

He swung the SUV around and headed away from Everly Plantation. I sighed, stretching my arms above my head, forcing the T-shirt even higher.

"Seriously, though,"—Brax glanced at me, then back to the road—"Cover-up. I'm trying to drive here."

I lowered my arms and tugged the hem back down. It didn't go far. "You know before when I said there was something wrong?" I kept my eyes on my knees.

"Mmmm?"

"Well, it's still there."

"What is? Are you in pain?" He threw a look my way.

Plucking at the hem of the T-shirt, I replied, "Yes. I'm in pain."

The SUV screeched to a halt, skidding on the road and throwing me forward until my seatbelt snapped me back into place.

"Ow! Brax, what the hell?"

His hands were all over me. "Where are you hurt?"

I grabbed his wrist and placed his hand between my thighs. "I'm in pain here." And I pressed him against my slickness. It was true. I ached. I ached so much it was almost unbearable. His breath hissed in through his teeth.

"You're not hurt, though?" he growled. "Just in… pain?" His fingers moved, stroked me, the scent of my arousal heavy in the confined space of the car. I groaned and arched my hips, inviting him to continue, to explore further, deeper.

"I ache," I panted, "so damn bad."

"Can't have that," he ground out, pushing a finger inside me, slowly withdrawing it to rub my own wetness against me, circle my clit, then plunge back inside.

I writhed in my seat, tugged my T-shirt over my

head, and tossed it to the floor. "Let me taste you!" I demanded, twisting in my seat and moving to my knees, careful not to dislodge his hand that was doing sinfully wonderful things to me, my hips rocking automatically.

"Katie." I didn't know if he meant to protest or encourage, but I was beyond words. Leaning over, I tossed his towel aside, revealing his cock, long and hard. Wrapping my fingers around the base, I slowly dragged my fist down the length of him and then back, before lowering my head and sucking him into my mouth. It was primal and potent, giving him pleasure this way, and with every long suck, I rocked forward and back, his fingers sliding in and out in perfect rhythm. Every thrust took me higher, and he was there with me, thrusting into my mouth until he pulled my hair, forcing me off him.

"What?" I grumbled, licking my lips and wanting more. With his hand still tangled in my hair, he kept my head still and kissed me, the mating of our tongues frantic and intoxicating.

"Come here." He lifted me over the center console, and I straddled him, the tip of his cock at my entrance. I wanted to prolong the moment, but at the same time, I wanted to impale myself on him, the unrelenting wave of desire overwhelming.

Tangling my fingers in his hair, I pulled his mouth to my breast, throwing my head back with a hoarse groan as he scraped the nipple with his teeth before soothing it with his tongue. And slowly, with sweat trickling between my shoulder blades, I lowered myself, felt the stretch as I adjusted to his size, his guttural groan echoing in my ears.

Our movements became faster, each growl answered by my whimper, each nuzzle met with goosebumps, and each scratch of nails met with a shudder. It was fast and furious, insane and merciless, but together, we climbed the mountain, reached the peak, and fell into blissful oblivion, hearts thundering in our chests, gasping for breath, blissfully content, sinfully sated.

"I don't know what's gotten into you, Katie Shelton, but I like it." His words dripped with satisfaction, and I smiled, my face buried against his neck.

The flash of headlights through the front windshield had my head snapping up.

"Shit," Brax muttered. Scooping the T-shirt off the floor, I pulled it over my head while Brax covered himself with the towel. A car door slammed, and I heard Brax wind down the window.

"You guys okay?" Jordan asked, and I slumped

against my seat, an uncontrollable urge to laugh coming over me.

"We're good," Brax answered.

Jordan placed one arm against the top of the door and peered inside, grinned wolfishly, then said, "You're looking a little…tousled there, Brax."

I burst out laughing. It was undeniable what we'd been doing. Christ, the scent of sex still lingered in the air, and Jordan was a dragon with unbelievable night vision. I was sure he'd copped an eyeful before we'd realized he was there.

"Nice of you to stop and check on us," I choked out, my chest heaving.

"That's me. Mister nice guy," he drawled.

"Jordan!" Rae yelled from the car. "Leave them be. It's not like we've never done the same."

"Oh, God." Brax wiped a hand over his face and turned torturous eyes to me.

"Let's just go," I told him. "We need a fresh set of clothes, and I'm famished."

"You shouldn't be, not after—"

"Jordan!" Rae screeched, cutting him off, and with a reluctant sigh and a cheeky wink, Jordan spun on his heel, returning to his car. Brax hit the button to wind the window up.

"In all seriousness, we need to regroup and

discuss what happened tonight. The Red Witch and Gunslinger know about Ridgeway—and they seem to think you're connected. We need to get ahead of this before it all goes south."

His reminder of what we were doing tonight, what was at stake, was a bitter pill to swallow. He was right—jumping his bones while on duty was not only unprofessional; it was dangerous. We were vulnerable. What if it hadn't been Jordan who'd come upon us but the Red Witch? Or the Gunslinger? We'd been oblivious, caught up in the rapture of each other. It was risky and stupid, and I couldn't believe I'd forgotten my training and had risked us both for sex.

"You're doing it again," Brax grumbled, turning the engine back on and continuing down the road. "Worrying. Beating yourself up. Blaming yourself. Flaming can be euphoric. You've never flamed before, and the first time can be a little disconcerting."

"Rae didn't say anything about this." I waved my hand, indicating my body, which once again had a frisson of blue electricity dancing across it. "I feel like I can't get enough, that I'll never be sated."

Reaching over, he entwined his fingers with mine. "It'll pass."

The rest of the drive to SIA was spent in silence. I was hyper-aware of the connection I felt with Brax, but the blue sparks of electricity slowly subsided as time passed. But not my awareness. Something told me that from this point on, I would always be super aware of Brax Lane.

EIGHTEEN

I spent too long in the shower, the hot water pruning my fingers, but I was sure I had rum leaking from my pores. Or maybe it was embedded in my nostrils because all I could smell was the overpowering scent of rum, and it was making me nauseous. Brax had offered to pick up a clean set of clothes from my apartment since he had to return to his hotel, anyway. I'd stayed at the SIA offices and showered there, borrowing a pair of Rae's sweatpants and a tank in the meantime.

Coming downstairs, I'd veered into the kitchen, following the alluring aroma of coffee, when someone started banging on the front door.

"Katie!" Duke shouted, "Katie, you in there?"

Flinging open the door, I eyeballed him. It was

four in the morning. What was he doing here at this time of day?

"Take it down a notch or seven, Duke," I grumbled, letting him in.

"Sorry. Wasn't sure you could hear me over all the reinforcements you've got going on here." His booted feet were loud behind me as he followed me into the kitchen.

"Coffee?" Holding up the pot, I poured myself a cup.

"Sure." Then he sniffed. Twice. "Is that smell you?"

"Rude much?" I grumbled, knowing my suspicions had just been confirmed. I still stunk like a distillery.

He pinched his nose. "What have you been doing?"

"Ha fucking ha." Shoving a cup of coffee at him, I pushed past, smirking when he spilled it on his shirt.

"Oh, I get it. It's one of those 'need to know' things. And I don't need to know," he said, following me into the main office area. Jordan and Rae were seated at their respective workstations, so Duke made himself at home at Brax's desk.

"You got it." Blowing on the coffee, I raised it to

my mouth and took a tentative sip. The jolt of caffeine was welcoming.

"What are you doing out here at this time of day, anyway?" I asked Duke, who'd now crossed his booted feet atop Brax's desk and was leaning back in the chair like he owned the place.

Blowing out a breath, he shot me a glare. "Well, since you've been ignoring my calls, I figured I'd come out here and tell you in person."

I automatically reached for my phone before realizing I didn't have it anymore; it had gone up in flames at the Everly Plantation. Along with my badge and pass card. Damn it. I scribbled a note to replace all three. And request another uniform.

"And you were calling because?"

He thumped his feet onto the floor and leaned forward. "I got a call tonight, something I thought you might be interested in."

"Oh?"

Rae and Jordan had remained silent up until now, but this had gotten their attention.

"Oh right, now you want to talk to me." Duke huffed, and I looked at him closely, saw the tight line of his jaw, the narrowing of his eyes.

"You were worried!" I barked, knowing I was

right when he winced. "You were worried I didn't answer my phone, so you came to check on me."

"Nawwww, that's so sweet," Rae teased.

"Shut up. So, I care about my friends, so what?" Duke crossed his arms, his discomfort apparent. I sobered. "Thank you, Duke, for checking on me," I said softly. "You're a good friend."

"Yeah, well, you're still alive, so my worry was misplaced."

Jordan's chair creaked as he shifted his weight. "Not entirely," he muttered.

"What's that?" Duke cupped a hand around his ear, but I held up a hand to prevent Jordan from repeating himself.

"You said you had news?"

"Yeah, yeah." Successfully distracted, Duke launched into his story. "So, I was at Stanley's tonight, and I got a call from someone wanting to procure a particular artifact, the Amulet of the Alliance."

Rae faked a yawn. "We don't need tales of your treasure-hunting adventures, Duke. Give us something real."

"Hey," he protested, "this is real. The Amulet of the Alliance holds the power of a coven of witches. Whoever wears it can harness that power."

"So?" This time Rae studied her nails. I knew she was feigning boredom. I'd seen her do this before, but the twinkle in her eye gave her away.

"So, Elva Petrov has commissioned me to procure the Amulet for her."

"And this is important to us why?" This time, Jordan chimed in, not understanding what Duke's commissions had to do with the SIA or our investigation.

"Oh my God, are they always this dumb?" Duke threw his hands in the air and turned to me. "You get it, don't you?"

I nodded. Oh yeah, I got it. Aloud I said, "Elva Petrov is a witch. She wants the amulet. Now, why would a witch want an ancient relic like that? Why now? And I'd imagine your services aren't cheap, Duke, so I'm guessing Elva is getting desperate?"

"Keep going." He grinned.

"I'd say she wants to protect herself from the Red Witch. That she isn't strong enough without the Amulet."

"Ding, ding, ding, give the girl a prize!" Duke hooted.

Rae interrupted his celebrating. "Wait, I don't get it."

"I suggest we bring Elva Petrov in and see what

she knows. She wants the Amulet for protection; my gut tells me it's related to the Red Witch, but,"—I held up a hand to silence Duke—"this is just speculation. She didn't specifically tell you that, did she?"

"Well, no," he admitted.

Rubbing a hand over my eyes, I glanced at the time on my monitor. "Guys, grab a couple of hour's sleep, then go visit Elva Petrov. Bring her here for questioning. She may not be a powerful witch, but she's still a witch, and the interview room has a dampener."

"Dampener?" Duke quizzed.

"Like a force field that subdues supernaturals' powers," I explained, smothering a yawn. "I'm gonna get some shut-eye too. It was a long night." I stood up, saying goodnight to Rae and Jordan, who preceded me out of the room.

Duke rested a hand on my shoulder. "You do look like shit, Shelton. And whatever you rolled in? That shower didn't take the stench away."

"Shut up," I grumbled, shuffling to the front door. I hit the button to open it, gasping in shock when Brax appeared on the other side.

"Snap." He grinned, indicating the swipe card in his hand.

I narrowed my eyes at it. "How do you have yours? Mine was totaled."

"Because I didn't take it with me. Kept my phone, keycard, and other non-essentials in the car." He glanced over my head. "Duke."

"Brax," Duke replied.

"Thanks for dropping by Duke. I'm fine, as you can see. I'm gonna have to get a new phone, though, so any updates can go through one of the others. Do you have Brax's number?"

"That's okay." Duke brushed past me. "I'll call Rae."

"See you," I called after him. He waved a hand, not looking back.

Brax closed the door. "What was that all about?"

I filled him in on Duke's latest commission and our unexpected lead.

"You think Elva wants the Amulet for protection?" Brax sounded surprised. "What if she's working with the Red Witch and wants it to bolster her power?"

"What we know of the Red Witch is that she doesn't work with anyone, and especially not witches. She destroyed her own coven for their power. I doubt very much that Elva is working with her."

"But you don't know for sure?"

"Okay, fine, I don't know for sure, which is why we'll bring her in for questioning. In a couple of hours, because right now, I'm done. I need some shut-eye."

"I'll join you." Brax followed me up the stairs and into the bedroom I'd claimed here.

"No sex," I warned him, "just sleep."

"I promise I'll be the perfect gentleman. Unless you request otherwise." His lips curled into a wicked smile as he stripped and slid between the sheets, stark naked. I swallowed, trying to ignore the potent response my own body displayed to his nakedness. Oh, who was I kidding?

Ripping my clothes off, I slid beneath the covers and reached for him. "Just a quickie then." I smiled against his chest. "And keep the noise down. Rae and Jordan are in the room next door."

"From what I recall, you owe them an earful anyway," he said, trailing his lips across my collarbone to nuzzle at my neck. I shivered in his arms.

"Good point." I smiled before surrendering to the tempestuous riot of desire that was already threatening to consume me with carnal bliss.

CHAPTER
NINETEEN

If I didn't know that Elva Petrov was a witch, I would never have guessed it. Goes to show that appearances really can be deceiving. Elva was tiny. So petite she could have passed as a child. And with a surname of Petrov, I'd conjured images of dark hair, yet Elva was so blonde, her short pixie hair practically glowed white. But her eyes. Man, they were so dark you could barely tell the pupil from the iris, and with her equally dark lashes and brows, it was a stunning combination.

She sat now in our interview room with her arms crossed. She hadn't appreciated being dragged into SIA offices this morning and, so far, was refusing to cooperate. Rae hadn't been able to get anything out of her, and I watched through the two-way mirror as Jordan took a turn.

Brax walked past, slapping my ass as he did so. "Coffee?"

God, yes. Two hours of sleep had taken the edge off, but was nowhere near enough for me to be fully functioning. I needed as much caffeine as my body could handle. "That'd be great," I said over my shoulder, keeping my eyes on Elva. Rae's phone began vibrating, and she looked at the screen before lifting it to her ear, then looking at me. I met her at the door.

"It's the lab. They've got your results." She handed me her phone, then closed the door.

"Shelton." Retreating to my desk, I looked at my screen, searching my emails for one from the lab.

"Got the results from those dirt samples you sent," the technician said. "We've run geothermal scans and can tell you that it appears the soil came from the Gawler Basin. Can't narrow it down any further than that, I'm afraid."

"Got it. Thanks."

"I've sent the full report via email; you should be getting it any second. There's something else you should know."

"Oh?"

"The Gawler Basin is where Section 27 is reportedly located."

That had my interest. "What's Section 27? That sounds military."

"It is. It's a highly classified military base for the development and testing of experimental aircraft and weapons."

"What? Like Area 51?"

"The rumor is, and this *is* a rumor, I have nothing official to back it up, but it is possible that Section 27 outgrew their location and moved to Area 51."

"So, Section 27 is closed?"

"Abandoned in 1968—reasons unknown. From what I can determine, it remains heavily fortified and off-limits. Most records are redacted, and despite further digging, I've been unable to discover anything more than what I've already told you."

"Okay, thanks, you've done great." Disconnecting the call, I leaned back in my chair and read his report, lingering over the words. Dirt from the Gawler Basin was found in Mrs. B's car. And Section 27 was located in the Gawler Basin. Allegedly. It couldn't be a coincidence. "What better place than an abandoned military facility to conduct experiments," I said out loud, jumping when Brax sat my coffee in front of me and kissed the top of my head. I hadn't heard him come in.

"What's that?" he asked, having heard me talking to myself. I told him what the lab had discovered, and he hurried to his laptop, pulling up a topography map and displaying it on the case board. We stood in front of it, my initial excitement waning. The area was vast, and with no coordinates, Section 27 could be anywhere within a two-hundred-mile radius.

"You don't think it's possible that all this stuff with the Red Witch and the Gunslinger…that's not a distraction technique, is it?" I asked Brax, my brow furrowing. "Because I don't buy that they want our help to stop Ridgeway. She's a shifter; she doesn't have insurmountable powers; the Red Witch could easily take her out."

"I think there is a lot more going on here than we know," Brax agreed. "The Red Witch had some interesting things to say about you. She knew about your daughter. Why would she even know that? And that Ridgeway wants to get her hands on you."

"When Paige was snatched in Redmeadows, they said they were planning on taking me. But then they discovered Paige wandering around unprotected and took her instead. And Elva Petrov?"

I played with the end of my hair, twirling it between my fingers as I thought out loud. "Is the Amulet of the Alliance pertinent? Because that sounds like something the Red Witch would be very keen to get her hands on. I'm thinking she's been leading us to Petrov the entire time, wanting us to retrieve the Amulet."

Brax nodded. "Then swoop in and steal it from us once we have it."

My eyes snapped to his as the pieces began to fall into place. Ridgeway was a means to an end for the Red Witch. "What about the Gunslinger?" I mused. "What's he doing here?"

"Hanging out with his ex?" Brax suggested. "Maybe they've reconciled. Or maybe he wants her to do something for him, something that needs more power than what she has, so she needs the Amulet to boost her magic."

"What could he be planning?" I began pacing back and forth in front of the case board. To one side were the animal attack victims that Rae had been working on. We were sure their deaths were due to supernatural causes. Vampires, shifters, ghouls, or a combination of all three. "The last time she did something for him, it was to spell Maxxan so vampires could walk in the sun."

"Right, but that was because of the Deadnettle crops, wasn't it? So, what if he's setting up again? Somewhere bigger. Needs a more powerful spell so his minions can withstand daylight, to tend the crops."

"Say somewhere the size of Section 27? That's rumored to be fifty square miles, if not more."

A smile slowly lit up his face. "Field trip?"

"Field trip," I agreed. "But first, we've got a witch who isn't talking. And I have a bad feeling that Duke is about to step into a whole world of trouble."

"How do you want to handle it?" he asked.

"You're more experienced than the rest of us in interrogation. Make Petrov talk. Send Rae and Jordan out here; we'll prep for the field trip."

Brax spun on his heel, and I listened as he made his way down the hallway. Minutes later, Rae and Jordan joined me, slightly dejected from their lack of progress with Petrov. I filled them in on the breakthrough and Section 27, which perked them up no end.

"Jordan, make sure the vehicles are ready to go. Enough fuel, water, and camping supplies. This won't be a day trip. Rae, log our plans with HQ," I ordered.

"What are you going to do?" Rae asked, swiveling in her seat to begin typing.

"I'm going into town to get a new phone and plant a tracker on Duke. We can't give him a protective detail, but we can keep an eye on him remotely."

"You think he'll find this amulet fast, then?" Jordan asked. "You think he knows where it is already?"

"Duke is a man of many talents, and finding ancient artifacts is right up his alley. He has a host of contacts, and I'm sure he has his finger on this particular pulse, so yes, I'm going to assume that it is only a matter of time before the Amulet of the Alliance is in Elva Petrov's witchy little hands. And then the Red Witch will strike. We have to prevent that, but we also need to get Ridgeway. This has gone on long enough. I think somehow the Red Witch got wind of what Ridgeway is up to and is using it to her advantage."

"You think she's playing us?" Jordan asked.

"Most definitely," I replied, snatching up my car keys and a new swipe card. "I'll text you with my new cell number. Give me a list of what supplies you need from town, and I'll grab them while I'm there."

CHAPTER

TWENTY

Fitting a tracker onto Duke's truck had been easy. Planting one on him personally had been a little challenging, but I'd managed to slip one into his wallet when he left it with his keys on the bar. Yes, we were at Stanley's, and yes, it was ten in the morning, but in my own defense, we were drinking coffee. Strong, black, wake-me-the-fuck-up coffee.

"You're sure about this?" My concern was genuine, and my face reflected it when Duke returned from the bathroom.

"What? Getting the amulet? Pft, that's easy," he assured me. I looked at his face, the strong, handsome face of a good friend. It niggled that he was being dragged into this.

"You know where it is? Already?" Surprise colored my voice.

"Got a strong lead, yeah. But this one is going to take me a while due to distance."

"Oh?"

"Peru."

"Right." I studied my coffee cup as if the answers to the questions of the universe could be found in the dark liquid. I was glad I'd got the tracker into his wallet because the one on his truck was now useless. He wouldn't be driving to Peru.

"Shelton?" Duke leaned sideways and nudged me with his shoulder.

"Yeah?"

"You look like shit," he told me.

I choked out a laugh. "Yeah? Well, I look better than you." Knocking back the rest of my coffee, I stood and slapped him on the back, hard, like he did to me. "You be careful out there—if you die, I'll kill you."

"Ditto."

I headed back to my truck, reeling when I opened the door, and the stench of stale, fermented rum escaped. Next on the agenda, another shower. And body scrub.

It was midday by the time I returned to the SIA offices, my skin tingling from the torture it had received in Paige's shower. I'd used all of her almond and coconut body scrub, but at least I no longer smelled of alcohol. I'd packed a backpack with the essentials, bought a new phone, and was back in my second skin, my SIA uniform. I'd stopped by the store and purchased the camping supplies Jordan had requested, and as I pulled up, he met me at my door.

"You get everything?" he asked, holding the door open for me.

"Sure did." I jerked my thumb to the bed of my truck.

"Sweet."

Hopping out and slamming the door, I headed toward the house, then stopped and swiveled. "How did it go with Petrov? She still here?"

"Brax released her. I assume he got what he needed, but he said he's not talking till you get back."

Heading inside, I paused in the hallway while my eyes adjusted to the dimmer lighting indoors.

"Oh good, you're back." Rae brushed past me,

carrying a large box. "We're almost done loading up the vehicles, and then we'll be ready to head out."

"Cool. I'm good to go." I indicated the backpack I'd slung over my shoulder. "Jordan is sorting through the supplies I picked up in town. We'll head out in a few minutes. Where's Brax?"

She nodded toward the conference room, and I looked at her in surprise. We hadn't used the conference room yet, had no need to. What was Brax doing in there? Opening the door for Rae, I waited until she'd passed through before joining Brax.

"I hear you had success with Petrov?"

He was leaning on the huge conference room table, studying a map he'd laid out on it. Glancing up, he smiled. "I'm satisfied." He nodded.

"Do tell."

Straightening, he looked up at the ceiling as if recalling his interrogation with Petrov before speaking. "She swears she isn't in cahoots with the Red Witch, but she had heard via another coven that the Red Witch is looking for the amulet. Petrov's plan is to get the amulet first and use it against the Red Witch."

"Ballsy move." I was surprised. The petite little witch would be pulverized by someone as powerful as the Red Witch.

"I thought so. She has a backup plan, though. If she can't use the amulet against the Red Witch, then she plans to trade it."

"In exchange for what?"

"Immunity."

I nodded, impressed. "Smart witch." Moving around to stand by his side and study the map, I asked, "This is Section 27?" He'd outlined an area with a yellow highlighter pen.

"Yeah, the Secret Service doesn't have much intel on it either, so this isn't one hundred percent accurate, but I believe Section 27 is within this radius."

"I'd imagine it's still protected? Guarded, you think?" I studied the map. The area he'd outlined was on the edge of the desert, a mountain range along one border.

"I doubt there are active personnel. I've requested satellite imagery for heat signatures, but I'd say they'd have electronic surveillance. Fences— most likely electrified. Possibly landmines. Anything to stop anyone from getting too close."

"We've got equipment to get past all of that."

"Me too." Folding up the map, he shoved it into one of the pockets of his cargo pants. "Ready?"

"Yep." I was turning away when he stopped me. "Wait, Katie."

"What is it?" I asked.

He didn't answer. Instead, he kissed me. This kiss felt different from all the others, not that they'd been bad. They'd been epic. But this kiss was soft, poignant, full of emotion, and I felt it. Everywhere. Even my hair tingled.

"Brax." I broke the kiss and moved back. That kiss had been full of love, and despite how he made me feel physically, I wasn't sure I could go there with him. I wasn't sure I could put my heart on the line again. We were about to head out on a dangerous mission, and... he stopped my train of thought by placing a finger over my lips. I frowned.

"Shhh. I can hear you thinking from here. Overthinking, if we're being honest. I just want you to know that as long as you want me, I will be by your side."

"Right," I whispered, more confused than ever. He chuckled, winked at me, then led the way out of the conference room. I followed behind, silently assessing what the hell had just happened. He'd surprised me by *not* confessing his undying love.

Outside, three vehicles were lined up, ready and waiting.

"Three?" I directed my question to Jordan, standing by the open door of Rae's flatbed truck.

"We need to take Bear with us. But we also need all of our supplies, and those fill up two vehicles on their own. Rae and I will go together. You and Brax can take the four-wheel drives."

I nodded in agreement and opened the door to the front vehicle. "Brax, do we have coordinates?" I'd need to punch them into the GPS, or we'd be driving blind. My phone vibrated, and I glanced at the text message—Brax had sent the coordinates. "Smartass." Hauling myself into the driver's seat, I slammed the door and buckled in. This was it. I could sense it, feel it in my bones, that we were heading toward something big. Ridgeway had been several steps ahead of us the entire time, but now I felt like we were finally catching up—that we were in with a shot. Gunning the engine, I waited, watching in my side mirror while Brax climbed into the four-wheel-drive behind me, and Rae and Jordan settled into the flatbed. I grabbed the radio and pressed the button. "All set?"

"Let's do it," Jordan replied, followed a second later by Brax's curt, "Affirmative."

Releasing the handbrake, I eased out, ignoring the feeling of unease that settled over me with each mile we put between Maxxan and us. The landscape changed the further we traveled, and soon I saw the same red dirt I'd found in Mrs. B's car, confirming what I already knew. We were on the right track.

We'd been traveling for over five hours when the radio crackled and Brax's voice filled the cab. "We should set up camp for the night," he said. "There's a clearing up ahead, to the left."

"Gotcha," I replied, taking my foot off the accelerator and slowing. Tall, gray trees bordered the road. How anything survived out here was beyond me, but I guess the plant life had adapted to the desert-like conditions. I saw the clearing Brax mentioned and turned in, driving the four-wheel drive around in a large circle before killing the engine. My neck and shoulders ached, and I stretched, easing the kinks and knots.

The other two vehicles pulled up, and I covered my nose and mouth from the dust cloud that came with them.

"We made good progress today," Brax said, joining me where I leaned against the front bumper of my vehicle. "I've calculated that we'll reach Section 27 around lunchtime tomorrow."

"And then the fun begins." Pushing away from the bumper, I flung open the back door and hauled out my sleeping bag and backpack. "The temperature is going to drop tonight," I said to no one in particular. "We're going to need a fire for warmth, so gather as much wood as you can."

We got busy setting up camp. Soon a fire was blazing within a circle of rocks, sleeping bags rolled out, a pot of water suspended over the fire. I was dying for a coffee, and it seemed I wasn't the only one, judging by the grumbling coming from Rae.

"I hate camping." She slapped at a mosquito, then another. "Did I mention that?"

"Only like a thousand times." Jordan rolled his eyes.

"Yeah, well, I don't do camping. I do plumbing. And electricity." She slapped herself in the face, and I laughed, dug around in my backpack, and tossed insect repellant at her.

"Use this. Seems they like you."

"Don't know why," she bitched. "You'd think my blood would be all dark and twisty, not something nice to drink."

"Maybe they like dark and twisty," Jordan soothed, spraying some insect repellant onto his hand and running it over the back of her neck.

"You like dark and twisty." She lowered her chin to her chest while he massaged her neck.

"I love dark and twisty," he flirted, and she leaned back in his arms, her face reflecting her bliss. I looked away only for my gaze to collide with Brax, who was watching me across the campfire. I arched a brow in query, and he shook himself, as if he'd been daydreaming, then busied himself with the can of now boiling water, pouring some into the cups lined up with coffee and the rest over the freeze-dried dinners we'd packed. Mmmmm. Gourmet.

We drank our coffee and ate our dinner while night fell around us. It was eerie and creepy and strangely beautiful at the same time. I was used to the darkness. At Grandma's, we didn't have streetlights, and when night fell, it was dark like this. Grandma had often lit a fire out in the backyard and let us roast marshmallows over it when we were kids. A smile tugged at my mouth from the memory.

"I'm turning in." Brax startled me. I'd been so lost in my memories. "I suggest you all do the same. We'll hit the road at sunrise."

I didn't know what I was expecting, that he'd suggest we zip our sleeping bags together, maybe? So color me surprised when he wriggled into his bag, turned his back to the fire, and for all intents and purposes, appeared to fall asleep. Slowly I followed suit, pushed down the feeling of pique that he hadn't wanted to sleep with me, and tried to get some shut-eye. Morning would come all too soon, and we still didn't know what awaited us at Section 27.

I awoke to something tickling my neck. Opening my eyes, the first thing I saw was an arm wrapped around me. Brax was in my sleeping bag, curled lengthwise along my back, hips touching mine. The tickling was him pressing kisses onto my skin.

"Morning." His lips brushed my ear, and I shivered.

"What are you doing?"

"I would have thought that was obvious." He chuckled, lifting his head.

"I thought you didn't want to sleep with me?" My emotions were all over the place, conflicting emotions, and I didn't know how to deal with them. I felt like I'd been on a roller coaster ever since I met him, and yet all along, he'd remained steady, both feet planted firmly on the ground, my rock.

"There has never been a time when I did not want to sleep with you," he growled, "but if I'd crawled in here with you last night, we would have done more than sleep, and I didn't want to embarrass you in front of your family."

A smile curled my lips, and I stretched. Rolling to

my back, I looked up at him. "Look," I said quickly, "I never meant for things between us to get this far. We work together. But after we've brought down Ridgeway, we'll go our separate ways. You're Secret Service. After this job, there's no need for you to hang around Maxxan."

He stared at me silently for several moments. "Afraid I can't agree to that," he finally answered. Brax reached over and stroked my face. "I can't just let us go our separate ways, Katie, because I am in love with you. I love you."

My mouth fell open, and my mind briefly blanked. Then I found my voice.

"No, you don't."

He let out a snort and dropped his hand. "You know, that is one truly annoying habit you have, telling me how I feel. I know my own mind. And heart."

"But you've only known me a short time!"

A slight smile curled his lips. "I began to fall in love with you the moment I laid eyes on you. And each day that passes, I fall further and harder, and I know that you're scared, so I backed off, but today? Today you need to know, before we throw ourselves headlong into danger, exactly how I feel."

"Brax..." My eyes were wide at his revelation. He

leaned over and kissed me. A long, deep kiss filled with promise and passion. I loved the way he kissed me, as if he were a drowning man and I was his savior.

"It's okay." His mouth slid down to nuzzle my neck. "You don't have to say it. I know it's fear holding you back. I'm a patient man; I can wait."

CHAPTER
TWENTY-ONE

The overhead sun blazed down, burning my skin and drying my eyeballs. I groaned and lifted my arm to shield my face. Something wet dripped from my hand onto my cheek, trickling over my lips. Instinctively, I licked, then frowned. Blood. I tasted blood.

I groaned, the slight sound rasping in my throat. *What was wrong? What was going on here?* My ears were ringing; I couldn't hear anything over the internal noise. Turning my head, I squinted. *Where was I?* Slowly, the horizon took shape. That's right. Section 27. We'd found what we thought was Section 27, only there had been nothing here. No buildings, no airstrip, nothing but goddamn red dirt.

Brax and Jordan had been huddled over the map

spread out on the hood of Brax's SUV, pointing and jabbing, arguing. Rae was fooling around with Bear, and I'd walked ahead, hands-on-hips, studying what was meant to be Section 27. My boot came down; there was a click. I froze. Everyone froze. That click had been so soft, yet we'd all heard it.

"Don't move!" Brax had shouted, yet it was too late. I was in a forward momentum. I couldn't stop my body from moving, despite anchoring my boot to the ground. I toppled, I fell, and the mine exploded.

I didn't feel pain. I blinked in blessed relief. Thank god I didn't feel pain, for I sure as hell just blew my damn leg off. I was too scared to look, but I was alive, so I could flame and heal myself, but not armed as I was. Wriggling on the ground, I began unbuckling my belt, throwing it away from me, digging in my pants for my phone, tossing that too.

Shadows formed overhead, Brax leaning in close, cradling my face. I pushed him away in irritation. This was going to hurt soon. Real soon. I didn't have time to reassure him. I had to get anything dangerous away from me, and I had to flame. He knew from the frantic movements of my hands, but then the pain hit in a giant wave of agony. It lifted me up and body-slammed me into the ground. Through the ringing in my ears, I heard my own scream.

"Help get her weapons off," I heard Brax shouting, then multiple hands were on me, tugging at me. "I'm sorry, this is gonna hurt." Brax hauled me upright and pulled my shirt up to get at the extra gun I had tucked in the waistband of my pants. I had weapons all over. A blade inside each boot, the gun in my waistband, not to mention the standard holster I'd already gotten undone and tossed. The world spun so fast my fingers dug into the dirt to try to hold on.

"There, there, she's done," Brax panted, laying me down. "Flame, Katie, you're okay, just flame."

I turned my head, saw Brax stripping out of his clothes; knew he must be injured too. He needed to flame. Just as I did. Closing my eyes, I summoned my fire, breathed in a gulping breath as it consumed me, took the pain away, and healed me before spitting me out the other side, restored and naked on the ground.

"Here." Rae tossed me fresh clothes while she scooped up my weapons. I was wobbly, but whole. I watched as Brax flamed a few feet away, awed by the magnificence of it. I'd never seen someone flame before and had to admit it was pretty cool. He looked like a phoenix rising from the ashes, all majestic and godly. And then his flame went out, and he was naked, and I still couldn't drag my eyes away. For Brax to be injured while the others weren't meant he had to have been heading my way when the mine exploded. He'd been prepared to put himself in harm's way for me.

Jordan tossed him his backpack, and Brax grabbed it, pulling out fresh clothes.

Rae snapped her fingers in front of my face, a knowing grin on her mouth. "How are you feeling?"

"Yeah. Good." I cleared my throat and accepted the bottle of water from her. "Booby trap, eh? So, we were right. This is Section 27."

"Assholes," Rae grumbled, taking a swig from her own water.

"Yeah, well, now we have something to work with," Jordan said, scooping something off the ground and holding it up to study it. "We have a piece of their mine. Something that Bear can scent."

"You think he could?" Rae asked in surprise.

"I think it's worth a try. For them to plant mines around here means we're close. There has to be something more, something we're not seeing."

Within minutes, Brax and I were once more suited up. Only I was missing a boot. I'd packed extra clothes, not extra footwear, and what was left of my left boot was nothing but a scrap of leather.

My problem was compounded when Jordan said, "I think it's better if we go in on foot."

"You're right," Brax said. "They'd be expecting vehicles. We go in, single file."

"Errr. Guys?" When they turned to look, I pointed to my foot, minus its shoe.

Jordan shook his head. "She won't get far on that."

"Not a problem," Rae piped up. "She can ride Bear. In fact, we all can. It'll be faster. And he's a hellhound; he can carry us all easy."

Brax ran a hand around the back of his neck. "It could work. But we'd need detectors, and he'd need to take it easy. I've seen him when he's on the scent, and that hound is fast. We need to be able to detect the mines."

"But that could work in our favor," Rae protested. "Even if he triggered a mine, he's moving so fast we'd be out of the blast zone before it went off."

"Risky," Brax argued, not looking convinced.

"We don't have a lot of choices here," I cut in. "I say we go for it. On the proviso that Bear can get something off that piece of shrapnel." I nodded toward the shard of metal Jordan was holding. "If he can't, then slow and easy it is."

Within minutes we were on Bear's back, and Rae was leaning forward with the piece of shrapnel. Bear huffed and slobbered, then took off, so fast I wrapped my fingers in his fur and hung on for dear life. Just as quickly, we stopped again, so suddenly that we bumped into each other, and Rae toppled forward over Bear's head, landing on her ass in the dirt with a thump. We'd traveled approximately two hundred yards.

"What the hell, Bear?" Climbing to her feet, Rae dusted off her butt and eyeballed the hellhound, who decided now would be a good time to sit. Jordan, Brax, and I slid down his back and landed in an undignified heap.

"Yeah, well, that worked. Not." Brax reached out a hand and hauled me up.

"No. He got the scent," Rae argued, "but he either lost it, or it ends here."

Jordan waved his hands around, indicating the vast nothing surrounding us. "Here? But there's nothing here."

"Pft. Have some faith," Rae scolded. Reaching up, she stroked Bear's snout. "Where is it, Bear?" she crooned, scratching behind his ears. "Where did it go?"

Bear barked, the sound echoing and making the ground tremble before he stood and began pawing at the ground.

"It's underground!" Of course, why hadn't I thought of it sooner? If you were trying to hide something out here with nothing but vast open spaces, you'd go underground. "There's got to be a trapdoor or something. Brax and Jordan, you've got the metal detectors. See what you can find."

Within seconds Brax and Jordan were scouring the ground we stood on, and sure enough, the metal detector went off...right beneath my feet. Dropping to my hands and knees, I began scooping the fine red sand up in my hands and tossing it aside. The others joined me until we'd revealed a large steel door.

Rae sat back on her haunches, face covered in sand and sweat. "How do we open it?"

"You don't." Brax dug in the cargo pocket of his pants, pulling out a tool that looked similar to a screwdriver—only it wasn't. "I do. Move out of the way."

It took time, but eventually, Brax picked the multi-barrel lock, and he and Jordan heaved the door open. It was huge, big enough to drive a car through, and with it standing open, we could see inside. A ramp leading beneath the earth.

I hesitated in the opening, peering inside. Lights flickered on as soon as we opened the door, but that wasn't to say this place wasn't booby-trapped. They'd planted mines outside to keep people away, and it would be foolish not to proceed with caution.

"Here." Brax handed me a black box, and I looked at it quizzically. "Use it to detect infrared beams. I doubt they've planted mines or bombs inside their facility, and I couldn't detect any triggers on the door itself. So, hold this out in front of you, press this button,"—he pressed my finger down on the red button in the middle of the device —"and keep it pressed. Then move forward. Slowly."

I did as instructed, holding down the button and moving forward. No infrared beams detected, so I kept going, one step after the other, bare feet silent.

It was cool in the tunnel, and as we progressed further in, the lights would flicker on ahead of us. But something was glaringly wrong. "Why aren't there alarms? Why aren't there cameras?"

"I think there used to be." Jordan pointed, and I followed to where he was looking, where I could see the remains of an overhead camera, now just a bunch of wires dangling from the roof.

"You think Ridgeway and her gang disabled them?" Rae was sweeping her flashlight left and right, the extra beam of light picking up broken switches on the wall and another camera.

Brax nodded. "Makes sense. They want to use this place; they'd have to disable all the military safeguards put in place."

"But wouldn't the military know? That they have intruders who'd dismantled their security measures?" It puzzled me. "Unless...Ridgeway has someone on the inside, someone on the military who would turn a blind eye. Maybe even gave her the information about Section 27 in the first place."

"The ghouls could be involved," Brax said, coming up close behind me and making me jump.

"Distinct possibility," I agreed, screwing my nose up at the thought.

We lapsed into silence as we walked through the long tunnel. It curved twice and seemed to go on forever. I wished now we'd brought our vehicles, for the tunnel was indeed big enough to accommodate them, but we'd come in on foot, and it was taking longer than I'd anticipated. We must have walked a mile already when the tunnel opened up into a large dome-shaped room. It was huge, the size of a football field. In the center was a structure similar to a dock, with a crane and a hut set on the top. On the opposite side of the dome were two more tunnels leading off in different directions.

"Great," I sighed, taking a swig of water. "Which way now?"

"Let's go see what's in the building up there." Brax led the way. "I'm assuming this is some sort of loading station; it's big enough to accommodate trucks and their cargo. There may be a map or directions."

Jordan dropped back. "You two go. Rae and I will stay down here. Keep an eye out. The military safeguards are down, but Ridgeway wouldn't have left herself unprotected."

Brax and I headed up the staircase. The room on the platform at the top was unlocked, and judging by the amount of dust, no one had been there for a long time. There was a single desk with a rotary phone, an office chair that leaned precariously to one side, and a shelf with cupboards beneath it running the entire length of one wall.

"Damn," Brax muttered, standing with hands-on-hips as he surveyed the room. "There used to be a map. Look—you can see the discoloration on the wall." He was right. Someone had torn down the map.

I peered closer. "Yeah, but look here." I traced my finger over the wall where the map had been. "Pinholes. Not just at the corners, but here. And here."

Standing shoulder to shoulder, we compared the two pinholes to what we knew of the layout outside. "The tunnel to the right." He said it under his breath, but I heard him. Turning my head to answer, I stopped, drinking in the sight of him. Being this close to him was distracting. It made my blood sizzle and pulse pound, but I was getting used to these sensations, equating them with him.

"You need to stop looking at me like that." He turned to face me, sliding a hand around the nape of my neck. "Because if I do what your eyes are telling me you want me to do, then you're going to get embarrassed when Jordan and Rae bust in here when the building starts shaking."

I giggled, then slapped a hand over my mouth. I didn't *giggle*. Heat flamed my cheeks red, and Brax laughed. "You're so cute when you're flustered." He dropped a kiss on my lips and stepped back. "Hold that thought, Shelton. We're going to kick Ridgeway's ass, and then I'm all yours."

TWENTY-TWO

We took the tunnel to the right and hit pay dirt. Eventually. It was another couple of miles of walking when the terrain changed. Small tunnels started branching off the main one, and we came into another large open area. It was a veritable city beneath the ground. Laneways ran parallel to each other and, on either side, buildings. What looked like golf carts were scattered around, but we had yet to see movement.

"This has to be it," Rae whispered. We'd hunkered down behind an abandoned truck, its tires flat.

"Agreed," Jordan replied.

An unnerving feeling of panic swept over me.

This was it; this was my mission, I had to lead my team on this, and suddenly I was awash with doubt. What if I got them hurt? What if Ridgeway got away? I wasn't prepared for this. What was Nate thinking putting me in charge?

"Take a breath." Brax's mouth was at my ear, and he rubbed a hand up and down my back. "You've got this. You're ready. What do you want us to do?"

Sucking in a lungful of air and holding it, I squeezed my eyes shut tightly. Sweat prickled my skin, and I thought I might puke.

"Katie, breathe." He nudged my shoulder, reminding me to expel the breath. I did. And with it came clarity. Nausea and doubt receded.

"We need to split up," I whispered. "Search each laneway, meet at the end." I pointed. "At the building with X8 on it. And we will systematically search each lane until we find something. Do not enter any buildings; note where it is and report back. We'll go in together."

It took over two hours searching the laneways, but we didn't come up empty-handed. Rae discovered fresh boot prints on the stoop of one of the boarded-up buildings. We met at the end of the lane and cautiously made our way to the building in question.

"You're right," Brax said, examining the boot prints. "Not fresh, fresh, but someone has been here." He rubbed his chin. "Probably within the last few weeks."

"Any signs of surveillance?" I asked. I hadn't identified any cameras or motion sensors. Neither had my team, for they all shook their heads. "Right, let's go in. Brax, can you get the door?"

We waited while Brax picked the lock, then stepped inside, single file, weapons drawn. The room was empty except for furniture and a stack of archive boxes. I walked over to them and examined the writing scrawled on the front. Dates. Going back five years. The most recent box on the top was dated last month.

Lifting it down from the pile, I put it on the table and tore off the lid. Inside were files and reams of data, a jumble of numbers that held no meaning to me. But the files looked promising. Lifting one out, I flicked it open and scanned the page.

"What is it?" Brax looked over my shoulder, reading with me.

"I think it's patient files." Closing the folder, I pulled

out another and then another. "These are the records of her experiments." None of the files had names; she'd allocated each person a number, and that was how they were referred to—all but one. I couldn't miss the file with the name Shelton scrawled across the top.

My hands shook. I knew what this was. This was Paige's file. When they'd taken her and injected her with their foul concoction, the mixing of DNA to create a super paranormal. All her patients had died as a result. All except for Paige. The paper crackled as my hands curled into fists. I couldn't hold the file steady, so I laid it on the table and spread the pages out. Brax, Jordan, and Rae gathered around and read with me.

"Jesus." Jordan straightened, his hand reaching for Rae, who was frowning.

"I don't understand," she murmured. "Does this mean...?"

"There has to be another file." My voice was devoid of emotion; my heart barely beat in my chest. For in the file was my name. Words like *"the continuation of the experiment. Excellent results, Katie Shelton."* Yet I hadn't been taken; I hadn't been injected. I'd remember. But something had happened. I was connected somehow, and the answer was in these files.

"Start searching the boxes," Brax ordered, closing the file and tossing it back into the box.

Systematically, we went through the files, but I knew where to look. I had a feeling of such intense trepidation that it couldn't possibly be leading me in the wrong direction. "Four years ago. Search the boxes from four years ago."

"Why? Did you remember something?" Brax asked.

I shrugged. "Four years ago, I was pregnant with Abigail. There were lots of appointments, scans, bloods. And the birth was difficult. I could have been compromised at any point."

Brax plowed through the boxes, tossing them aside until we found the one we needed. He slammed it onto the table and tore off the lid, then hesitated. Slowly, he lifted out a file with my name on it and handed it to me. Opening it, I began to read, blinking when the words blurred, not noticing the tears rolling down my cheeks.

The others remained silent, waiting. I finished reading, closed the file, then my eyes.

"Katie?" Rae whispered, reaching for me, but Brax held her back.

"Wait," he said.

I cleared my throat and opened my eyes, but I

couldn't look at them, couldn't face the pity I knew I'd see on their faces. Instead, I focused on the file.

"So, it appears Ethan was part of the experiment. One of the earlier adaptions that were successful. And when he got me pregnant with Abigail, that made her...us...part of the experiment, too. It was planned. Clinical."

"Wait! What?" Rae screwed up her face. "So Ethan was a mutant? I thought he was human."

"It says that he was a fire demon. He fooled me too." My breath hitched in my throat. He'd tricked me. Fooled me into thinking he was human, that he loved me—and our daughter. Instead, we were nothing but an extension of Ridgeway's crazy experiment.

The wave of hurt that washed over me wasn't unexpected, but in some ways, it was cleansing. A relief. It made it easier to let him go and move on. But my daughter? That they'd done this to my daughter? That was unforgivable, and the anger that warmed my blood and narrowed my eyes was fast building to a rage that could destroy worlds.

Brax wrapped a hand around my nape as if to hold me steady, yet I wasn't moving. Maybe he knew I was about to explode; go on a rampage so dark and devastating I'd never return from it.

"Let's take a minute. This is a shock. Do you mind if we read the file?"

"Go ahead." I didn't care; it was mostly medical jargon and some photos, an ultrasound of Abigail. It didn't say anything in the file about the betrayal, that our relationship had been fake. But they'd died? Had that been part of the plan, too? Put them in a life-or-death situation and see if they survived?

Snatching up the file, I flipped through, looking for evidence. But it appears their deaths had been unexpected and unplanned. The car accident had been just that. An accident. Although there was speculation that Abigail should have been able to flame to heal herself. Morons forgot she was a nine-month-old baby with no such instincts. She'd been asleep in her car seat. She didn't wake up. Something cold settled in me and spread, overriding the grief and the pain.

"It's time," I growled, "time to take Ridgeway down. And I'm going to be the one to do it. She's mine."

TWENTY-THREE

My pyre gun was in my hand; I had another in the waistband of my pants, blades, and other deadly goodies jammed into my belt. We'd grabbed a golf cart and followed the tracks down a tunnel, Brax behind the wheel.

We had the element of surprise, and we used it well. Ridgeway and her crew had no idea we'd discovered Section 27, breached the underground facility, and made it all the way to the medical facility housed hundreds of yards beneath the red soil.

Now, as we rounded a corner, my mouth curled at what lay before us. The building was one level, with a red cross on the front. And lit up like a

Christmas tree. We'd hit pay dirt. She was here. A guard stood at a metal door; a machine gun slung across his shoulder. He hadn't seen us yet, the golf cart moving almost silently across the ground. Brax glanced over at me and nodded. Ready. With the gracefulness of a jungle cat, he slid from the seat and rolled, ducking low and sprinting to the side of the building. Rae and Jordan followed. I moved to the driver's seat, and with a savage grin, I hit the gas.

The cart surged forward, and the guard avoided being run over by leaping onto the hood. Immediately, he punched through the windshield and tried to grab me, but I was ready with my gun, hitting him directly in the chest. Blood bloomed, and I ducked under the steering wheel while the buggy crashed into the doors of the medical facility. The screech of metal was deafening as the cart punched a path into the building. Without hesitation, I leaped through the shattered windshield and rolled off the hood, gun in hand, ready to shoot anything that moved.

Brax was right behind me, and together we swept the foyer, but it was empty. Lowering his weapon, he snaked out a hand and curled it around my nape, pulled me toward him, and kissed me.

When he ended the kiss, he gave me an unblinking stare.

"When it is time, no matter what we find, I want you to unleash everything you have in you. Hold nothing back. You've got strength, and I want you to use all of it. Give in to the rage and let it feed you. Kill anything that stands in your way. Remember, if they're here and not restrained, then they're Ridgeway's, and they're your enemy."

"I'm ready." Mentally I threw my conscience down a dark, deep well I would fish out later. Assuming there was a later.

Then we heard it. The sound of booted feet running in our direction. They were coming.

"Brax." I gripped his hand, and my eyes screamed everything there wasn't time to say. He squeezed back and gave me a devilish smile.

"Hold that thought, Katie. I intend to collect on it."

With a gun in each hand, I squared my shoulders. A snarl of vengeance tore from my throat, and my eyes blazed as Ridgeway's men burst into the foyer, opening fire on us. I saw the fangs and knew they were vampires, impossibly fast and extremely lethal. Keeping cover behind a reception desk, I fired, taking down one, then another. There were so many of them it became a blur, and they were upon us. Brax grabbed the shoulder strap of a machine gun and whipped it around the neck of the nearest vampire, and with a merciless jerk, the vampire's head snapped off, and Brax whirled to tackle the next one.

Keeping out of the line of gunfire from Rae and Jordan, who had taken shelter behind the golf cart, I joined Brax, sinking my blade into the back of a vampire who'd been about to jump him from behind. I slashed and gouged his heart, shredding it, before pulling out my knife and searching for my next victim.

Launching myself airborne, I practically flew across the room and landed on another vamp. Silver flashed and buried into his heart, and with a twist, I finished him. I was knocked off my feet by a punishing blow and pitched forward. Using the momentum, I curled my body under, and my attacker sailed over my head. None of them were prepared for my speed. As soon as he'd hit the wall, Rae or Jordan, I'm not sure who, shot him.

More were coming. We were outnumbered, but they hadn't anticipated the rage fueling me. Grabbing a body from the floor, I hauled it up and used it as a shield. Fangs that were meant for my neck tore into dead flesh instead. The next few minutes were filled with body-to-body combat, gunfire, and silver blades. Instead of tiring, I was euphoric. My fire demon exalted in the thrill of the hunt. And then the vampires began to scatter. They sensed their impending defeat and made a fatal mistake. Turning their backs on us. I unleashed silver throwing stars, rapid-firing them into their hearts. *Take that, motherfuckers!*

With the vampires scattering, Brax and I headed down the corridor they'd come from. I caught a glimpse of Ridgeway and a small man, who I assumed to be Leroy Byers, sprinting away from us.

"Ridgeway!" I snarled. "I'm coming for you!"

Ridgeway turned her head with a look of disbelief. Byers didn't. He just ran faster. They reached a door, fumbled frantically with a keypad before the door opened, and then slammed shut behind them. I reached it, slamming my fist against it and pulling at the handle. It was reinforced.

"Stand back. I've got it." Brax pushed me aside and then slapped something onto the lock. Explosives. I curled into the wall opposite, and Brax wrapped himself over me, protecting me from any shrapnel from the blast.

"Okay?" he asked, his eyes running over me, searching for signs of injury.

"I'm good. You?" I panted, blue electricity sparking from my fingertips.

"All good. Let's do this!"

Side by side, we burst through the doors; guns drawn. Ridgeway and Byers cowered behind what appeared to be a cryogenic chamber in the middle of the room.

Byers shot his hands into the air. "I give up," he squeaked, "I surrender." Brax shot him, and my mouth fell open as Byers hit the floor, a hole in his forehead spilling blood.

"What the hell?" Ridgeway rasped, stepping back to avoid the pool of blood from getting on her shoes. I glanced at Brax. *Yeah, what the hell?*

He shrugged and glanced my way, saying, "Sorry, babe. I've got different orders than you. SIA likes to bring them in alive. The Secret Service? Not so much."

I hesitated, then nodded. "I'm okay with that."

"What?" Ridgeway screeched, suddenly realizing her predicament. "No. I'm unarmed. You can't shoot me."

"I've got no reason not to." Brax kept his gun on

her, but didn't pull the trigger. "Who's in the deep freeze?"

Her lips tightened into a straight line; then, her head cocked as if considering.

"If you kill me, you'll never get him back," she said.

"Who?" God, she had balls, massive ones, so bold as to try to negotiate with us, with Brax, who had just demonstrated his intentions of shooting a ray of pure energy through her skull.

She reached a hand into the pocket of the white lab coat she wore and Brax swore. "Easy. Don't try anything stupid," he warned.

"Relax. I'm not armed," she drawled. I couldn't get over how not freaked out she was. Paige had been right: Ridgeway was one cold-hearted bitch.

She pulled out a phone. "May I?"

"What, call for help? No, you may not. Give." Brax stepped forward and snatched the phone from her. She kept her hands in the air, but the smile curling her red lips was pure evil.

"I have a little...insurance policy," she said, "if you care to go to the messages marked 'Duke.'"

"Duke?" I seized on the name. She didn't mean my Duke, did she? Duke Ellis, whom I'd planted a tracking device on since he'd accepted a commission to retrieve the Amulet of the Alliance. While Brax did as Ridgeway requested, I pulled out my phone and opened the tracking app. What I saw froze the blood in my veins.

"You didn't." My voice was icy calm, but my heart thundered in my chest, and I could feel my demon ready to launch at her, to tear her limb from limb.

"I did." She smiled, and I shot her.

TWENTY-FOUR

Ridgeway fell to the floor, clutching her shoulder, blood pouring between her fingers. It wouldn't kill her, but it would hurt like hell.

"You shot me!" Her eyes widened, astonished.

"Restrain her," I told Brax, holstering my gun and turning my attention back to my phone screen. The good thing about a tracking device was it told me exactly where Duke was. About fifty yards from here. She'd taken him. She'd taken my best friend. I prayed that she hadn't injected him with her DNA-changing concoction yet.

"Go," Brax said, holding Ridgeway's phone up. I glanced at it. On the screen was a photo of Duke tied to an examination table, a gag over his mouth, and a look of fury in his eyes.

"Wait!" Brax held up a hand, then aimed his gun at Ridgeway's head. "Is the Red Witch here? Or the Gunslinger?"

"What? No." Ridgeway shook her head, pushing herself along the floor and away from Brax. He followed, standing over her.

"You'd better not be lying. Because I won't kill you. I'll just make you wish you were dead."

At that moment, I couldn't have loved him more. It filled me, from the top of my head to the tips of my toes. I was full of love for this man. My heart sang with it, and I touched a hand to my chest in wonder.

I shook myself out of my stupor when Brax turned to me. "Be careful, okay? Be on the lookout. Also, as an extra incentive for Ridgeway..." He stepped over her body to the cryogenic chamber and shot the control panel. The gentle hum that had been coming from the machine slowly faded to nothing.

"Nooooooo," she cried, crawling on her hands and knees toward the unit.

"Whoever's in there doesn't have much time," Brax said, his tone light, "so you'd better pray Katie gets back here with Duke real fast."

I cast a glance at the unit, curious beyond measure as to who was inside, but with Brax damaging the controls, I guess we'd find out soon enough. Turning on my heel, I sprinted out of the room. I watched my phone screen as I kept running until I busted into a room further down the corridor. As suspected, Duke was tied down to the table. His head turned toward me, and he began making noises behind his gag.

"Duke!" Sliding my phone into my pocket, I rushed forward, fingers fumbling with his restraints.

Gunfire erupted from behind me. I spun, and the bullet meant for my chest tore through my shoulder instead. Duke had a guard, one I hadn't noticed when I burst through the door. He fired again, hitting me in the leg. I fell, momentarily stunned by the impact and cursing myself for stupidly rushing in like that.

I reached for my holster, but the guard was over me, a gun aimed at my head.

"I wouldn't," he said. I closed my eyes for a moment, the throbs of pain from the bullets almost paralyzing me. "Down on your knees. I've got you at gunpoint. Ridgway's going to love this," he crowed. "She's been wanting another Shelton."

I didn't move. If I didn't return, Brax would

come looking for me. Seconds ticked by, and I knew what the guard was thinking. He thought I was dying. He thought I was bleeding out on the floor. Duke was thrashing on the table, yelling beneath his gag, his words muffled, but I could take a guess at the language he was using. I just had to wait a little longer, not for Brax, but for Duke. I'd loosened the restraint on one hand. He'd be free any second, and all I needed was that distraction.

"Hey!" Bingo. I felt the breeze of Duke's hand as he reached out toward the guard, and in that split second, I charged at him, batting his gun aside to fire harmlessly into the wall. I snapped his neck before Duke had finished freeing himself from the table.

"Katie, you're shot. How bad is it?" Duke rushed toward me, an arm sliding around me to support my weight.

"I'm fine. Healing already." But I let myself lean on him because the bullet wounds hurt like hell. "Are you okay? Did they inject you with anything?" I ran my eyes over him, reassuring myself he was all right.

"Nah. I'm good. Where's Brax? I heard the gunfight."

"He's a few doors down. Come on; we'd better

get back before he kills Ridgeway. He's on a hair-trigger right now."

With Duke supporting me, we made our way back to the room where Brax had Ridgeway under gunpoint.

"You're shot!" Brax took in my injuries, his eyes blazing.

"My own fault, but I'm okay. I'll heal. Thank you for not killing her." I nodded toward Ridgeway, who was sobbing and hugging the leg of the cryogenic chamber.

Brax tossed his gun to Duke. "Keep that trained on her. If she moves, shoot." Then he kicked a chair over to me and commanded me to sit while he dug around in the drawers of a medical supply cupboard, tossing things onto the floor until he held up two bandages triumphantly.

"Who's in the box?" Duke asked, eyeballing the big metal tube that now had puffs of white rising from it. Whoever was inside was defrosting. I looked at Brax, who was crouched in front of me, wrapping my thigh in a bandage.

"Don't know yet. She's not talking. I'm guessing it's someone important—to Ridgeway, at least—and that damaging the controls wasn't a good thing."

"You murderer!" Ridgeway sobbed louder, hysterical in her grief. "You're killing him."

"What? Just like you killed all those innocent people in your quest for a super paranormal?" Brax drawled, continuing to administer first aid to my injuries.

"That was different. I didn't kill them on purpose. And if it had worked, they'd have power and strength beyond your imagining."

"Who is he?" I asked, trying to hide my wince of pain from Brax. "Husband? Boyfriend?"

"My brother!" she wailed. "He's my brother, and he has a rare genetic disease. I was trying to save him."

My eyes met Brax's in surprise. A shifter with a disease?

"Is he...human?" I probed, but she was shaking her head, tears mingling with snot and making a mess of her face.

"He's a shifter. I told you. It's rare. His shifter DNA is fighting with his human DNA. Killing him. There is no cure. It usually kills the host in infancy, but he survived. It was a late presentation."

"And you've had him on ice ever since while you tried to create a cure." Brax nodded, strapping my shoulder, softly stroking his fingers across my cheek when he was done.

Her story pulled at my heartstrings, but then I remembered my daughter and my heart hardened. "You had Ethan get me pregnant, purely for your experiment, didn't you?" My voice was flat, devoid of emotion.

Her head whipped up, and in that instant, the reality of all she had done showed on her face. She wiped her nose on her sleeve, and her bloodshot eyes met mine. I didn't say a word. Didn't have to. She'd changed my life forever, had taken my child, and the man I thought had loved me.

I watched as she touched the side of the cryogenic chamber, closed her eyes briefly in farewell, then launched at Duke. Duke stepped back in surprise. He didn't have a whole lot of skin in this game, and his instinct was to back away, not shoot her. Brax had no such qualms. Spinning, he snatched the gun from Duke, aimed, and fired. She jerked backward, red hair flying, then crashed to the floor, blood staining her white coat red.

"Sorry. I know you wanted her alive," Brax muttered.

I shrugged. "She had no intention of being taken alive. You didn't kill her. She committed suicide."

The room settled into silence as we each digested what had happened.

"Ummm," Duke broke the silence, "what do we do about this dude? Let him die or what?"

I stood and hobbled to the chamber, cupped my hands against the glass, and peered inside. "He was never meant to survive to begin with." I sighed. It was sad. But it also felt wrong to let him die like this.

"I know, I know." Brax holstered his weapon and began fiddling with the blown-apart controls. "Let's try to get this working, temporarily at least. What happens to him isn't our call. Katie, call your boss and see if he can arrange transport. Duke, go find Jordan. Between us, we can probably jerry-rig this to hold until help gets here."

Then it dawned on me. "You didn't shoot at that randomly, did you?" I pointed to where his pyre gun had fried the wires. "You did it knowing you had a reasonable chance of repairing it."

"Katie Shelton, you think you've got me all worked out." But the grin splitting his face gave him away. He'd shot the controls to put pressure on Ridgeway, not to be a cold and ruthless asshole.

THE CAVALRY ARRIVED. I'd called Nate, and he'd sent in a chopper to retrieve the cryogenic unit. Ridgeway's brother's fate was now in the hands of the SIA, although Nate said it would most likely be a decision the Council made.

Rae and Jordan were uploading data to the SIA servers and collecting any remaining pharmaceutical samples they could find.

Duke was chattering nonstop in my ear, and I finally turned to him with my hand in his face. "Shh," I said. "Give me a minute, okay? I have to find Brax; there's something I need to tell him. Why don't you go help Rae and Jordan?"

"Oh." He looked at me intently, then winked. "Right." Spinning on his heel, he left, and I went looking for Brax. I found him in the room where Ridgeway and Byers had died.

"I need to talk to you," I said from the doorway.

He glanced up, smiling when he saw me, then frowning at my blood-soaked bandages. "You need to flame."

"I'll do it later. It's fine."

"Katie."

I rushed to him and placed my finger over his lips. "I. Love. You."

"I love you too—" Brax replied, but I cut him off.

"No! Just…I love you. I said I love you. Me. Katie Shelton. But…" I sighed. "You traumatized me. You came here, you made me feel again, you made me love you, and I can't—I mean, I don't want to. I can't breathe!" I sucked in a gulp of air. "*Without you.*"

Gently, he cupped my face in his hands. "You can do this, Katie. We can do this. All you have to do is meet me halfway. All you have to do is say yes." He kissed me, achingly tender, then spun on his heel and walked away.

I let him go, jaw slack. I'd told him I loved him, and he'd walked away. Fury surged through me, and a spark shot out of my hand, igniting on the floor. Stamping it out, I stalked out of the room. He was right. I needed to flame. Limping down the corridor, I flung open doors until I found an empty room. Shutting the door, I removed my bandages, stripped, and then summoned my flame. It wasn't as bright as before. Calling on it again so soon had depleted my strength, but my bullet wounds were healed, and all that remained were small pink scars on my flesh. I could live with that.

Pulling my blood-soaked clothes on again, I threw open the door, then stifled a scream. Brax was standing on the other side.

Grabbing his shirtfront in my fist, I hauled

myself up to his face. "You changed my life. I don't ever want to live without you."

"Is that a yes?"

"Yes, it's a yes," I said, exasperated, then laughed when he scooped me up and spun me around in circles. And despite everything, despite all that I'd been through, the lies and secrets of my past, all the pain and joy, it had never felt so right as it did at this moment. He was mine, and I was his, and together we could have a happy life. My fire demon sighed in contented bliss.

The adventure doesn't end here. Ready for a devilishly good twist? Meet Lucifer like never before - she's a woman, and she's spectacular. Dive into the Hell's Angel series next and get ready to be captivated.

www.JaneHinchey.com/HellsAngel

Thank you for reading! If you enjoyed this book, I'd greatly appreciate your review.

You can find a complete list of my books, including series and reading order on my website at:

www.JaneHinchey.com

Join my newsletter here:

www.JaneHinchey.com/subscribe

And finally, join my readers group on Facebook here:

www.JaneHinchey.com/LittleDevils

Thank you so much for taking a chance and reading my book . It's readers like you who make this journey worthwhile and fuel my passion for storytelling. Your support means the world to me, and I can't wait to share more exciting stories with you in the future.

xoxo

Jane

FREE BOOK OFFER

Want to get an email alert when a new book is released?

Sign up for my newsletter today,

https://janehinchey.com/subscribe

and as a bonus, receive a FREE e-book of

Cupcakes & Curses!

READ MORE BY JANE

Find them all at www.JaneHinchey.com/books

The Ghost Detective Mysteries

#1 Ghost Mortem

#2 Give up the Ghost

#3 The Ghost is Clear

#4 A Ghost of a Chance

#5 Here Ghost Nothing

#6 Who Ghost There?

#7 Wild Ghost Chase

#8 Easy Come, Easy Ghost

#9 Life Ghost On

Witch Way Paranormal Cozy Mystery Series

#1 Witch Way to Magic & Mayhem

#2 Witch Way to Romance & Ruin

#3 Witch Way Down Under

#4 Witch Way to Beauty & the Beach

#5 Witch Way to Death & Destruction

#6 Witch Way to Secrets & Sorcery

The Gravestone Mysteries

#1 Fur the Hex of it

#2 Battle of the Hexes

#3 What the Hex

The Midnight Chronicles

#1 One Minute to Midnight

#2 Two Minutes Past Midnight

#3 Third Strike of Midnight

Clean Scene Inc.

#1 All in Vein

PARANORMAL ROMANCE/URBAN FANTASY

The Awakening Trilogy

Hell's Angel Trilogy

The Enforcer Series (4 books)

Standalones

Returned

Secret Fates

Destiny's Touch

Blood Cursed

Heart of Darkness

About Jane

Hi there! I'm Jane, crafting tales of paranormal cozy mysteries sprinkled with urban fantasy romance. Between sips of coffee and dodging my mischievous cats, I immerse myself in stories where magic meets everyday life.

Once known as Zahra Stone in the world of steamy urban fantasy, I've now merged those fiery tales under the Jane Hinchey banner. Off the page you'll find me binging on true crime documentaries or sneaking in a power nap. Dive into my stories and join me on an enchanting journey!

Find me here: www.janehinchey.com

facebook.com/janehincheyauthor

instagram.com/janehincheyauthor

amazon.com/Jane-Hinchey/e/B0193449MI

bookbub.com/authors/jane-hinchey

goodreads.com/jane_hinchey

www.ingramcontent.com/pod-product-compliance
Lightning Source LLC
Chambersburg PA
CBHW051256210726
48287CB00002B/522